DRESSAGE DREAMING

Horses Heal Hearts Series Book One

KIMBERLY BECKETT

SOUL MATE PUBLISHING

New York

DRESSAGE DREAMING

Copyright©2018

KIMBERLY BECKETT

Cover Design by Melody A. Pond

This book is a work of fiction. The names, characters, places, and incidents are the products of the author's imagination or are used fictitiously. Any resemblance to actual events, business establishments, locales, or persons, living or dead, is entirely coincidental.

Published in the United States of America by
Soul Mate Publishing
P.O. Box 24
Macedon, New York, 14502

ISBN: 978-1-68291-669-8

ebook ISBN: 978-1-68291-637-7

www.SoulMatePublishing.com

The publisher does not have any control over and does not assume any responsibility for author or third-party websites or their content.

To all of the horses who have enriched my life

over the past 30 years,

and to my very supportive husband, Tony,

and son, Chris,

this book is for you.

Acknowledgements

I would like to thank Pam Goodrich and my dressage trainer, Jennifer Grant, for their advice on the technical aspects of dressage and dressage competition. I would also like to thank my Beta readers, Kim Mallio and Donna Finlay, for their invaluable assistance. They found the gaps I didn't realize I'd left and made this story better. I would also like to thank the professionals in my life who have become dear friends— Joy, Beth, Debi, Jenn, and Diana. Finally, I would like to thank *New York Times* bestselling author Grace Burrowes, without whose advice and encouragement I would not have been able to accomplish this first novel.

Prologue

The day could not have been more perfect. The sky was clear and blue, and the sun was shining brightly. There was just a hint of a breeze blowing on a warm June day in London as the four members of the British Olympic dressage team stood together on the raised pedestal to receive their gold medals. As he bent his head to allow the Olympic official to put the medal around his neck and shake his hand, Michael Stafford closed his eyes briefly to savor the moment. When he raised his head again, he was beaming, and hardly noticed the fragrant bouquet of flowers thrust into his hands. His companions on the pedestal, Margaret Crawford, Jonathon Wells, and Roberta Randolph, were just as ecstatic and they embraced each other, smiled, and waved to the adoring and raucously cheering crowd. Michael scanned the crowd, and quickly located his fiancée, Emma Lockhart. Emma caught his eyes, grinned, and waved enthusiastically to him, then blew him a kiss. Michael waved back and winked to let her know he had seen her and understood.

"This is fantastic," Roberta shouted over the noise of the crowd. "I've never felt anything like this before." Michael had to agree. He had never felt more euphoric. The team had ridden their absolute best and the horses performed nearly flawless tests. They had particularly been worried about how Michael's stallion, Romeo, would react to the crowd noise and tension surrounding such a major event. He was high strung and hot under normal situations, but the Olympic Games were the pinnacle of competition and the stress levels were through the roof. Michael had to admit that despite the tension, he and Romeo had performed beyond his wildest expectations.

After the medal ceremony, the team was escorted back to the paddock area, and was immediately surrounded by their coaches, grooms, and family members waiting to congratulate them and share the moment. Emma was there, and came up to him to give him a congratulatory hug and kiss. He studied her radiant face as she stood back to savor the moment. At a little over five feet tall, Emma had hazel eyes, a pert little nose, and a lopsided smile that made it look like she was never quite serious about anything. She wore her dyed blond hair short, and, if Michael were honest with himself, wore a little too much makeup. Emma had to stand on her toes to reach Michael's six-foot two-inch height. He grinned as he bent over and whispered in her ear "As soon as this is over, love, I'll take you back to my flat and we can celebrate properly."

She smiled in return, nodded, and winked. "Absolutely! I can't wait."

Chapter 1

One year later

A loud, rhythmic banging noise shattered the glorious dream of his past Olympic glory, and Michael slowly woke and made the agonizing transition from perfect bliss to cold, stark reality. An earsplitting voice invaded his foggy, alcohol-dazed state "Oy! Mike! I know you're in there, man. Open up!"

"Bloody hell!" Michael groaned, as his head throbbed in pain. "Stop that pounding, I'm coming, I'm coming." Michael pulled himself up off the overstuffed leather sofa upon which he had apparently crashed sometime in the early morning hours after finishing off his last bottle of scotch. His mouth felt like it was lined with cotton, and his tongue was stuck to the roof of his mouth. His head was pounding in time with the beat of his heart, and his walk was unsteady as he took the first few steps toward the door.

The clock on the wall showed it was ten o'clock. Even the slow, steady ticking away of the seconds was painful to his head this morning. He gradually made his way to the door as he tried to mentally bring himself into the present. Now, a year later, Michael was living in the refurbished manor house on the farm in Surrey that he had purchased with the money he had earned as a result of his Olympic success. He had turned the small farm into a dressage training yard and boarding stable and christened it Stafford Oaks Farm. It was what he and Emma had dreamed of that night, the best night of his life. So much had happened since then.

As he moved toward the door, Michael scanned the compact living area that had once been the family parlor and noticed piles of dirty clothes and dishes strewn about the room. He hastily tried to move some of the worst of it out of the way. He gingerly opened the curtains of the window closest to his front door and squinted into the late morning sun to see who had so rudely awakened him. Lionel Hayes, his best friend for nearly twenty years and a fellow dressage rider, stood outside and peered back, motioning to the door. "Do you mind?"

Michael opened the door. "Lionel, you sod, what the hell are doing here?"

Lionel pushed his way into the room. He was a bit taller than Michael, but much thinner, almost gaunt in appearance. His blond hair and blue eyes were stereotypically British as was his long, thin nose, and prominent square chin. "I tried to call you on your cell phone an hour ago and you didn't call me back. I got worried. What in God's name have you been doing?" Lionel grimaced as he looked around at what had once been a neat and tastefully decorated manor. He wrinkled his nose "This is disgusting." Then Lionel noticed the empty bottle of Scotch on Michael's coffee table. "Now I know what you've been up to, trying to drown your sorrows in drink yet again. Well, my friend, it's not going to work, and I'm here to make sure you don't end up in the hospital with liver failure."

Lionel walked around Michael's home, opening curtains and cranking open several windows to allow a cool morning breeze to circulate through what had been a hot, stuffy home filled with dirty laundry and dishes and smelled like a cross between a men's locker room and a garbage dump.

"Look, Lionel, I think I'm entitled to an occasional drinking binge considering everything that's happened to me in the past year." Michael's mind immediately flashed back over the year that had passed since he had experienced the best day of his life: winning a gold medal at the Olympic Games held in his home country. Since that day, his life had been nothing but a series of setbacks and disappointment.

First, the owners of Romeo, the gifted stallion he rode to a gold medal in the Olympics, decided to take the horse out of competition immediately after the Games to make a tidy profit breeding him. Without Romeo, Michael wasn't able to continue to compete internationally, and was having a great deal of trouble finding another horse as talented to ride in Romeo's stead. Without the public exposure competition gleaned for him, his Olympic fame began to fade. His fiancée, Emma, who had enjoyed the glitter and attention he drew immediately following the Olympic Games, became bored with their lives after Michael moved out of the spotlight. It wasn't long before she began acting suspicious of his relationships with other women, accusing him of being unfaithful to her. Nothing could have been further from the truth, and he had tried to explain to Emma that he had to travel to teach clinics and market his skills as a trainer, but all she seemed to be able to see were the many women who clamored to meet him and get close to him. Her suspicions baffled him, because he took great pains never to be alone with any of the women he met through his clinics and loved Emma too much to cheat on her with any other woman.

Michael still wasn't sure exactly what had happened between them, but everything seemed to fall apart right after the Olympic Games. Before the Games, he and Emma were on top of the world, looking forward to a life together living on his training yard in the country outside London, where he would raise and train horses for himself and others in dressage, and she would continue working in the city for a prestigious law firm. He was certain they loved each other unconditionally, although he must admit in hindsight that their relationship wasn't perfect. Still, he felt betrayed, and had vowed to himself never to give his heart so foolishly ever again.

Michael picked up the tabloid from his coffee table and showed it to Lionel. On the cover was a picture of Emma with a one of Britain's most famous footballers. She was laughing and looking at him adoringly, and he seemed to enjoy her attention, smiling down and holding her close, with his arm around her waist. "I can't go anywhere without some reminder of Emma. While standing in line at the grocery store buying food for the week, I saw this in a rack next to the checkout line." He pointed to the photo on the cover. "It seems she has a penchant for rich and famous men," he said bitterly. "She used to look at me like that," Michael fumed. "Just wait until you get injured or retire, friend" he told the man in the photos, "she'll drop you like a rock." Unfortunately, although his head told him he had escaped a bad situation and should be grateful, his heart was still engaged, and he had tried last night to dull the pain with Scotch.

"Look, man." Lionel threw the tabloid back on the table. "You've got to let her go and get on with your life. You can't let her be your ruin."

Michael knew Lionel was right. His career and his life had gone seriously downhill since Emma left. While he had once been scrupulous about his preparation for public appearances and had always been punctual for clinics and lessons, he was now either late or, even worse, a last-minute cancel or no-show for fully booked weekend clinics for which he had already been paid half up front. He had also started to be chronically late for lesson clients, and one of his two working students had left him in frustration. As a result, the invitations to do clinics stopped coming, and many of his lesson clients moved on to other trainers. The agent he hired after the Olympic Games eventually dropped him. He had barely any income except for some horse boarding clients at his stable, and a couple of training clients who were also good friends and understood why he was acting out of character. Even those clients, though, were losing patience. As a result, he was becoming alarmingly close to financial ruin. He was barely able to make the monthly mortgage payments on his farm, and had been forced to live a very austere existence, the occasional drinking binge notwithstanding.

As Lionel moved a pile of clothes out of the way so he could sit down on the sofa, Michael's phone started ringing.

"Good God!" Michael groaned, as his head throbbed in pain. "What now?"

He picked up the phone. "Yes, what is it?" Michael growled into the receiver.

"Mr. Michael Stafford?" The clipped, and very formal male voice on the other line responded.

"Yes. This is Michael Stafford. Who is this?"

"This is Constable Eric Madden of the Surrey police. We have your brother Ian Stafford in custody here at the station."

Michael's heart sank, and he raked his fingers through his hair. "What has my brother done, Constable Madden? Why is he in custody?"

"Last night, your brother started a fight, and stabbed one of the patrons of the Rusty Nail Pub in Woking. The pub owner called us for assistance, and when two constables arrived in response to the Pub owner's call, he resisted arrest. He punched one of our officers before we were able to subdue him. He also had been drinking excessively according to witnesses at the scene. We have him in custody. Unfortunately, the man your brother stabbed died at the hospital two hours later, so Mr. Stafford has officially been charged with manslaughter."

Michael's heart sank. "My God!" he exclaimed. "That's simply not possible. Ian would never purposely hurt anyone unless he was defending himself." *Something must be seriously wrong if Ian had gotten himself into this kind of trouble.* "How is he, Constable?"

"He has a few bruises from the fight, and he has a pretty powerful hangover, but otherwise, he seems to be physically all right, and no one else was seriously injured," the constable replied. "He's asked me to contact you. He wants to see you."

"Certainly, Constable Madden. I'll be right there."

"Mr. Stafford, if I may, your brother has refused to speak with us about exactly what happened last night, and he has also not requested a solicitor to assist with his defense. I suggest you engage a solicitor to represent him at your earliest convenience. These charges are serious, and he may be facing life in prison if found guilty."

"Thank you, Constable. That's good advice. I'll get on it right away." Michael hung up the phone and looked at Lionel.

"I'm sorry Li, I have to go to the police station. It appears my brother Ian has gotten himself arrested, and could be in some serious trouble."

"Do you want me to come along? It might be nice to have some moral support."

"No, but thanks for the offer. This is family business, and I don't want you to get entangled in this mess. At least not until I get to the bottom of this."

"At least let me fix you something to eat while you shower and change. There's no way you want to go to the police station looking like you do right now." Lionel opened the refrigerator and searched for something he might be able to cook. "Do you have any eggs or milk?"

Michael shuddered at the thought of solid food hitting his much-abused stomach, but he knew Lionel was right. He needed nourishment, and scrambled eggs would work as well as anything.

"I do. If you look a bit, there should be both in there. Thanks, man." With Lionel now occupied in the kitchen, Michael turned and went into the bathroom. After Michael left the room, Lionel could no longer suppress the malicious grin he had been hiding since he arrived at Michael's home. His plan was working. He was, slowly and surely, ruining Michael Stafford's life.

Michael deserved it, of course. He had ruined Lionel's life during the British Olympic trials a year ago. Michael and Lionel had been friends since they were boys, both having a love of horses, and sharing that love by working odd jobs for Michael's uncle, who was a thoroughbred race horse trainer.

Although they went their separate ways after graduating Secondary school, they met again at the British Olympic Team trials. Both of them had competitive horses, and it looked to be a challenging competition. Lionel's horse was a talented off-the-track thoroughbred named Accolade he had trained with the help of his partner, Nigel. Accolade was great, but after a few less than stellar training sessions, Lionel believed his horse was exhibiting some residual lameness in his left front leg that wasn't responding to the approved methods of treating inflammation, so Lionel re-connected with one of his race track contacts and procured a corticosteroid currently on the banned substance list, to use on his horse. Lionel had gone out to the stabling area ostensibly to check on his horse, but instead was injecting Accolade with the steroid when Michael appeared and saw what he was doing. Lionel remembered the exchange like it was yesterday.

"Lionel, what the hell are you doing?" Michael demanded.

"Nothing. Accolade seemed to be a bit off this afternoon in training, and I just came by to give him an anti-inflammatory."

"There are very few anti-inflammatories that aren't banned for international competition. What is it you're using?"

"Never mind, it's something my home vet recommended for inflammation."

"You need to clear anything like that with the Team vet, you know that. I'll call him right away. You don't want to get in trouble for something like this."

"No, Michael, please." Desperation and fear were clearly evident in Lionel's voice.

"I don't know what you're up to, Lionel, but you jeopardize all our chances if you make the Team and you're doing something illegal. I've got to call the vet."

Michael did just that, and Lionel was ejected from the trials and any hope of competing in the Olympic Games. He left the Olympic trials in very public disgrace. Word of his disgrace made it to the press, of course, and headlines all over the country trumpeted his willingness to break the rules in order to succeed. Lionel's reputation was ruined. As a direct result of all the negative publicity, Lionel and his partner and lover Nigel Crawford's business suffered, and it became a chore just keeping their heads above water.

The reduction in income had seriously drained the couple's finances, and the stress took a heavy toll on Nigel's already ailing heart. Lionel watched helplessly as Nigel's health steadily declined. Lionel had taken him to specialists in an attempt to stop the decline, but it hadn't done any good. The only solution the doctors could offer was to find a way to reduce Nigel's stress, and Lionel was helpless to do anything in that regard. The reduction in income had seriously drained the couple's finances, and the constant stress caused by the relentless calls from creditors took a heavy toll on Nigel. One day, Lionel awoke to find Nigel's lifeless body next to him in their bed. He had died from a massive heart attack.

To add insult to injury, Michael had the nerve to attend Nigel's funeral. Their conversation that day was burned into Lionel's memory.

"Lionel, I'm so sorry for your loss," Michael had said, extending his hand.

Lionel had been tempted not to shake it, but decided that the others, who had been watching their exchange with interest, would have interpreted his gesture as petty and grasped Michael's hand in his own. "Thank you, Michael. Frankly, I'm surprised you came. You weren't particularly close to Nigel."

"I know how important Nigel was to you. Lionel, and I wanted to be here to support you in your grief."

Not knowing how to respond to that statement without cursing, Lionel quickly changed the subject. "Congratulations, by the way on your success at the Games. You deserve all the acclaim you've been getting. You should be very proud."

"About that," Michael replied. "I'm also here to ask for your understanding and even your forgiveness for what happened at the Trials."

"Understand? Forgive?" Lionel barely contained his rage. However, he was again very conscious that the two of them had an audience. He ruthlessly schooled his features to mask his inner turmoil. Nevertheless, his voice was strained. "Your actions in turning me in to the authorities ruined my life, and I'm not exaggerating. I'm an outcast, a pariah in my own country, forever marked as a cheater and a fraud. It will be some time before I ever even consider forgiving you, much less understanding your actions. We were friends, Michael. Did that mean nothing to you? You could have easily looked the other way, and no one would have been the wiser."

"If you believe that, you're incredibly naïve. The drug testing used by the authorities nowadays is so sophisticated that I have no doubt they would have found out about your drugging Accolade. You would never have gotten away with it, and when they eventually discovered that I knew and didn't turn you in, your actions would have brought me down, too. And what if you had felt you had to do the same thing at the Olympic Games? Discovery there would have led to not only your own disqualification, but also the disqualification of the entire team. You must see that I couldn't allow that to happen."

Lionel refused to accept Michael's excuse, and turned to leave. "If you'll excuse me, I have other guests to attend to. Goodbye Michael."

Lionel watched from the corner of eye as Michael, evidently disappointed by Lionel's response, left. Still appalled that Stafford had the nerve to even be here when his actions had been the cause of Nigel's death, it was then that Lionel made up his mind. Without Michael's interference, Lionel was sure he would have made the British Olympic Team, and have the medal that Michael now possessed, as well as all the fame, fortune and acceptance that went with it. As far as Lionel was concerned, the blame for Lionel's disgrace, his failing business, and Nigel's tragic death fell squarely on the shoulders of Michael Stafford.

From that day forward, Lionel plotted his revenge. The first step had been to contact Michael two weeks after Nigel's funeral to offer his apology for his behavior at the funeral, and to offer Michael his forgiveness and make an offer to renew their friendship. Michael accepted him with open arms.

Chapter 2

Michael stood at the bathroom sink and looked in the mirror. "My God, old man," he told his reflection, "you look bloody awful." He gazed critically at his reflection and saw his brilliant blue eyes were bloodshot from lack of sleep and alcohol, his thick, wavy black hair was sticking up all over the place, and a day's growth of beard covered his square chin. Right now it was hard to imagine this was the same man that had been crowned "Britain's Sexiest Man" in a magazine article published soon after the Games. Now, at thirty years of age, the reflection in the mirror frightened him more than a bit. He mentally shook himself out of his reverie. There was no time to waste contemplating his reflection. All he could do now was pull himself together and try to figure out how to get Ian out of this latest scrape. Heaven knew this one seemed much more serious than anything Ian had gotten into so far.

He turned toward the tub and started the water for a shower and slowly removed his clothes. As he stepped into the shower, and stood under the blessedly hot stream of water, he considered how much his life had changed in the past year, and how much he needed something positive in his life. He needed to get a hold of himself and get his life back on track. Ian needed him, and he had to be able to step up and support him. If only the stars would align, he could compete one of the horses he already had in training to a level that would attract the attention of a wealthy patron who could afford to buy him a horse to compete on the international stage once again. Only then could he afford to keep his farm and his dreams for a future career training and riding horses in dressage, the sport he loved.

Michael's thoughts turned to his brother, Ian. Michael had to admit that Ian was a different man since his tour with the British Army in Afghanistan, but deep down, he was still the Ian he had grown up with and loved. There was nothing he wouldn't do to help him now when he needed him most.

All of those years as children, when Michael had taken care of Ian while his parents ran their restaurant in Brighton, came back to him in a rush. He had always been responsible for keeping Ian out of trouble, and those habits die hard. Even as adults, Michael felt responsible for keeping Ian safe. After his return from Afghanistan and subsequent honorable discharge, Ian had temporarily moved in with Michael until he was ready to find a place of his own. Now, Ian had gotten himself into some very serious trouble, and Michael, admittedly through his own recklessness and irresponsibility, didn't have the financial wherewithal to help.

His shower finished, Michael toweled himself off and dressed. He went out to the barn to let his barn manager, Tiffany, know he was going into town. As he searched the stable for Tiffany, Michael slowed his pace and took some time to listen to the sounds of several horses pleasantly munching their hay, gently snorting and occasionally stamping at flies as they consumed their breakfast, and noticed the air was filled with the sweet, inviting smell of horses, fresh hay, wood shavings, and the more pungent odor of fresh manure.

Brilliant sunlight was streaming into the barn from skylights he had insisted be cut into the barn roof to allow as much natural light as possible into the horses' stalls. At the time, it had seemed an unnecessary extravagance, but this being England, the land of clouds, fog and rain, Michael wanted his stable to be as light and airy as possible. Today, the effect of the bright sunlight on the fine mist of sawdust and hay dust kicked up as the barn workers swept the aisles clean created a halo effect that sparkled in the sunlight and gave the stable a magical feel. Michael's breath caught. It had been ages since he had taken time to just wander through the aisles and absorb the atmosphere in the company of his horses. This few minutes taken in their presence calmed him like nothing else could. He took a deep breath, closed his eyes, and felt centered for the first time in weeks. After what must have been just a few seconds, but felt longer, Tiffany's voice interrupted his reverie, and he located her, informed her he was leaving for a while but didn't provide her any more details, then drove to the police station.

Michael had lived in Surrey for only a year, and in that time he had never had the need to visit the local police station. The particular station that was holding Ian was located in the town of Guildford, a twenty-minute drive from Michael's farm in Cranleigh. The building was small, but Michael could see that despite the historical exterior, the inner workings of the station were very modern. He quickly located the reception desk, and purposefully approached the desk officer. "Excuse, me, Constable. I'm Michael Stafford. I'm here to see my brother, Ian."

"Of course, Mr. Stafford, right this way." The officer took a set of keys off of a hook behind the desk, opened a door to the left of the reception desk and indicated that Michael was to follow him.

The officer took Michael down a long corridor, through a door, and into a separate area with four ten-foot by ten-foot cells. Michael spotted Ian lying on his back on a cot in one of them, his fingers laced behind his head on the pillow, staring at the ceiling.

The constable spoke to Ian. "Your brother's here, Stafford."

Ian looked over at Michael from where he was laying, and slowly, gingerly swung his legs over the side of the bed and winced as he raised himself to stand beside the bed. "It's about time you got here," Ian growled. "What took you so long?"

"You should be grateful I'm here at all," Michael responded. "You look like hell."

Ian was normally a handsome but ruggedly built young man of twenty-seven, equal in height to Michael with an aristocratic nose very similar to Michael's with the exception of a slight bump in the middle where it was broken when a viciously kicked football had hit him in the face as a youth of ten. He had the same blue eyes as Michael, but instead of their father's raven black hair, Ian had their mother's sandy blond locks. Ian had never had any problem attracting female attention, and his time in the service, with its demanding physical requirements, had only increased the attraction as he developed a muscular, body-builder-like physique. This day, however, Ian definitely looked like he had been in a barroom brawl. His left eye was black and blue and swollen nearly shut, his lip was split and had been bleeding, and his jaw had a bruise on it. Michael could also see that Ian's knuckles were scraped and bruised. It was clear to Michael that it was difficult for Ian to stand up straight without grimacing in pain. He wouldn't be surprised if some of Ian's ribs were bruised, or even broken. Ian walked stiffly over to where Michael was standing.

"What happened, Ian?"

Ian looked over Michael's shoulder at the constable, who nodded slightly and stepped away, moving closer to the door to allow the brothers some privacy. Ian sighed and beckoned Michael to come closer to the cell. He grabbed the bars of his cell with both hands and bowed his head, gritting his teeth in frustration. He spoke softly in case the constable had stayed within hearing distance of the brothers. "I didn't go to the pub to make trouble, Michael, I swear it. I had gone to the pub to get something to eat, and had a beer, just one beer, mind you, with my meal. There was a group of four blokes about my age that started harassing a woman at the bar. She kept telling them to leave her alone, but they just kept after her, until one of them grabbed her arm, and started trying to drag her to the back of the pub. She got away from him, and slapped him. It looked like he was going to hit her back, and no one else seemed to care what was happening, so I decided to intervene and do something to help her."

"They obviously didn't appreciate my intervention, and remember there were four of them. One of them drew a knife and threatened me with it. I had my Army knife in my boot for protection, and I took it out to get them to back off, but one of them snuck up on me from behind and pinned my arms, another tried to take the knife. I struggled against the man holding me, managed to break loose, but his sudden release made it impossible to stop my right arm from moving forward. My knife caught the man in front of me in the belly, and he fell immediately. Two of his friends drove him to the hospital, but the fourth convinced others in the pub that I was dangerous, and that they should help him detain me. After they bound me, he and others knocked me around a bit. In the chaos that followed, I looked for the woman to make sure she was okay, but she was nowhere to be seen. I assume she was able to get away. Then the police arrived.

"Unfortunately, the blokes were locals and the pub owner thought them good enough customers to back up their story that I started the fight, and that I had threatened them with my knife. They even convinced the constables that I was drunk and dangerous, since I had so brutally stabbed their mate. I tried to tell them that I was only defending myself, but they didn't believe me. They even roughed me up a bit before handcuffing me. The woman could have backed up my story, but she was gone."

Michael realized immediately that Ian's case was going to be difficult. "We'll have to see what we can do to find her. She may be the only eye witness that isn't biased against you. She's the key witness to support the fact that you acted in self-defense. First, though, we have to get you out of here."

"The sooner the better. I have a splitting headache, and I think one of my ribs is broken."

"He's being charged with manslaughter," the constable intoned. "You'll have to post bail to take him out of here." Michael tensed. The constable had reappeared at Michael's back without him noticing. Hopefully, Ian had noticed his presence and not revealed the woman's existence for the constable to hear. If the men who had beaten Ian found out the woman might be available and willing to testify, they might try to find her and do something to convince her she should stay quiet.

"How much will bail be?" Michael recovered sufficiently to ask the constable without any strain in his voice.

"The magistrate has set bail at fifty thousand pounds, due to the seriousness of the charge. He will also have to appear here regularly to ensure he hasn't left the jurisdiction, leave us his passport, and there's a good possibility he will have to wear an electronic monitoring device on his ankle so we can make sure he doesn't leave the jurisdiction until trial. He will most likely come up for trial in six or eight months."

"Fifty thousand pounds!" Michael said. *It might as well be a million.* He quickly composed himself and responded to the constable with what he hoped was an attitude of confidence. "I don't have that kind of money with me now, but I'll be back as soon as I can with the funds. Is there any way in the meantime he can be seen by a doctor? I'm concerned about his condition."

"We have a doctor on call in case we need him for emergencies. I don't see this as an emergency, but I'll see what I can do." The constable led Michael back out to the desk area, and Michael waited while the constable made a phone call. When he was satisfied that the doctor would be out to the station soon, Michael left to see what he could do to get Ian out of there.

His first call was to his parents. His mother answered the phone after just two rings.

"Hi, Mum," Michael said. "How are you?"

"I'm fine, and your father says hello. How are you, Michael, and more importantly, how is Ian doing?"

Michael sighed. "Actually, that's why I'm calling. Ian has been arrested and charged with manslaughter. He got in a fight in a nearby pub, and killed a man with his knife. He swears it was self-defense, and I believe him, but the police aren't convinced, so they've got him jailed until we can raise fifty thousand pounds for bail."

"My God, Michael! My poor Ian. Is he all right?"

"He's been better, I'm sure, but he's all right for now, though he has some visible cuts and bruises, and he might have at least one or two broken ribs. What worries me most is that I don't know how long he'll be able to live in a cell the size of a large closet without losing his cool." Both Michael and his mother knew that Ian had been diagnosed with Post Traumatic Stress Disorder upon his return home from service with the Army in Afghanistan, and had been exhibiting symptoms that worried them both. As a result, Ian had moved in with Michael and was helping his barn staff clean stalls and turn out the horses as a form of therapy. He had also started seeing a National Health Service therapist in Guildford that specialized in treating military veterans with PTSD, for more intensive treatment.

"Don't worry about the bail, Michael," his mother replied. "Your father and I will think of something. It's critical that you get him out of that cell as soon as possible."

"Agreed," Michael said. "Are you sure you have the money to do this? I wasn't sure business was doing as well recently as it had in the past."

"We have been contemplating taking out a loan for some improvements to the restaurant, so we have some of the loan documentation already filled out. We can use the money for bail instead. The improvements can wait. Besides, if Ian remains in the area for trial, we will get the funds back."

"All right. Send me a text message when you've wired the funds and I'll post bail and get him out as soon as I can. When I get Ian home, I'll have him call you so you can speak with him in person and let him tell you himself that he's all right."

"Thank you, Michael. You've always been there for Ian, and your father and I are grateful. Ian is too, although he will probably chew nails before he tells you that."

Michael chuckled into the phone. "You're right about that. Taking care of Ian comes naturally after all these years. Now, I have to go. Remember to text me when you wire the money."

"We will, Michael. Take care."

"Bye, Mum. Talk to you soon." Michael hung up and checked his phone for any messages from Tiffany, then dialed the number for the solicitor he had used in the past for business matters, Rodney Rogers. If Rogers didn't have the expertise for the case, he would surely know someone who could.

Michael made an appointment for later that day, then, knowing there was nothing more he could do for Ian until he met with the solicitor and posted bail, Michael's thoughts turned to his farm and his future. Lionel was right. It was time to stop mourning Emma's betrayal and move on with his life. He had some good training clients, but neither of the two young dressage prospects he had purchased in an attempt to train his own competition horse had turned out to be capable of performing dressage at the international level.

A cursory conversation with the solicitor's assistant as he had made his appointment indicated that to defend someone accused of murder, fifty thousand pounds was just the beginning. Adding to that the fact that the solicitor would have to hire an investigator to find the mysterious woman Ian identified as his only possibility for acquittal, and his expenses would be even higher. Without hope of further financial support from his parents, Michael had to find a way to make a large amount of money and soon.

The only way he had ever earned any money in his life was through dressage. He knew the probability of lightening striking him twice with the kind of luck that led him to find Romeo and his owners at just the right time to benefit them all, was slim to none. Nevertheless, he still had hoped he could compete internationally again. Without money or a sponsor, though, his hopes were equally slim. The longer he was without a competition horse, the harder it would be to get back in the game.

Michael called Lionel and asked him to meet him at a local restaurant and pub for lunch. After being seated and ordering some beef and potato pasties and only water to drink, though Michael could have done with something stronger, Lionel started to explain why he had initially tried to contact Michael. "I have good news. I've heard there's a stallion available for sale that sounds a lot like your Romeo."

"Unfortunately, he was never *my* Romeo, but you definitely have my attention," Michael responded. "Tell me more."

"Roberta called me earlier this morning after she tried your number and didn't get an answer. She told me that she heard that the German rider, Hermann Wolfe, was getting disappointing results from the Mendelssohn stables' premium stallion, Tempest. It appears that Mendelssohn himself has decided to take the stallion away from Wolfe, and is looking for a new rider. He has even made it known that the stallion may be for sale to the right buyer."

"That is news." Michael couldn't help feeling hopeful, even excited, as he contemplated the possibility that he might have a shot at being the new rider for Tempest. He had heard great things about the horse, but also had heard rumors that Wolfe was not the right rider for him, and wasn't succeeding on the show circuit as expected with the immensely talented young stallion. "How do I get in the door with Mendelssohn?"

"Actually, Roberta knows one of the trainers at Mendelssohn's breeding and training facility near Hamburg. She told me she would be happy to put in a good word for you and help you arrange an appointment and test ride." Seeing Michael's stunned look, Lionel grinned. "You know we all want you to be successful, Michael. What Romeo's owners did to you after the Olympics was unconscionable after all you did to make that horse a star."

Michael secretly agreed with Lionel, but he couldn't make that statement out loud. "Please tell Roberta how grateful I am for the opportunity she's arranged for me. I can't thank her–or you for that matter–enough."

"Don't mention it," Lionel responded. "Roberta has a link to a YouTube video of Tempest, so let's take a look."

They went back to Michael's home and watched the video on Michael's television. Tempest was truly a remarkable horse, with great gaits and tons of personality, but it was clear that Wolfe wasn't the rider for him. The stallion appeared tense at times and it was clear that Wolfe wasn't riding him in a way that allowed the stallion to shine. "I'm sold, Lionel." Michael was trying to rein in his excitement, but it was difficult not to show his enthusiasm now that he had seen the video. "Let's set up an appointment for a test ride and plan a drive to Germany as soon as possible."

"You've got it," Lionel replied. "I want to be there when you ride this horse."

Chapter 3

It was 6:00 AM on a school day, and Jessica Warren was in a hurry to get her sister Hailey up and out of bed so she could dress and get to school on time. "Up and at 'em, Hails." Jessica had poked her head into Hailey's bedroom and turned on the light. "Time to get going. I have to get you to school and to the airport to meet Liz by eight."

"It's too early to get up," Hailey groaned sleepily. "Can I sleep just another five minutes? Debbie said she'd pick me up for school today, so you don't have to drive me."

"Sorry, Hailey, I still need you to get up and get ready on time. I'm on a tight schedule. Do you need some help?"

"No, I'm fine. Thanks, Jess."

If Jessica had been honest with herself, she would have to admit that Hailey has been taking care of herself without much help for most of the last five years since the accident that killed their parents and crushed both of Hailey's legs so severely that they had to be amputated below the knee. At seventeen, Hailey was now a junior in high school, and about as well adjusted as any average teenager. Jessica credited much of Hailey's confidence to the therapeutic riding program that Jessica's dressage trainer and mentor Elizabeth Randall had started several years ago, as well as the dedication of the many doctors and physical therapists that Hailey had working on her case since the very beginning. Jessica was especially grateful for the extra help of their neighbors, the Turners, who had taken the girls under their wing after the accident. Jessica couldn't even count how many times she had relied on Bill and Betty Turner to look in on Hailey when Jessica had to work late to keep watch over a colicky horse, or spend entire weekends at horse shows out of state.

"If you need anything, just let me know," Jessica said.

Jessica watched Hailey struggle to maneuver her wheelchair down the narrow hallway between her bedroom and the bathroom to take a shower and couldn't stop the overwhelming feeling of guilt that hit her like a physical blow. It was her fault Hailey was suffering, and Jess knew with every fiber of her being that she would do everything she could to make Hailey's life better. That was the reason she was traveling to Germany - to find the horse that would help her to become an international success and ultimately through that success, earn enough to be able to support Hailey and provide for her as she deserved. Jess knew she could never give Hailey her legs back, but she could make her life better than it was right now.

When Hailey finally made it into the bathroom, Jessica started making breakfast. While Jessica fixed eggs and toast and started a pot of coffee, Hailey finished her shower and maneuvered herself back into her room to dress. By the time the food was done and the coffee brewed, Hailey was dressed and ready to eat.

"Jess, is there any way we can get me better quality prosthetics?" Hailey asked. "It's very difficult for me to get around and into and out of the bathroom the way things are now."

"It's on my list of things to do as soon as I can save up the money. You know Mom and Dad only had basic medical insurance coverage, which didn't cover more than the most inexpensive prosthetics. You'll just have to get by with a wheelchair or crutches with your current prosthetics until I can earn some more money. The good prosthetics are pretty expensive."

"I know, Jess. I just wanted to make sure you knew."

"I know, Hailey. It just takes time to save that kind of money."

"You're right. I'm sorry, Jess." Hailey understood that Jess was doing everything she could to make her life easier, and felt guilty that she was causing her worry once again. She decided a change of subject was in order. "So, tell me about this trip," Hailey said. "What are you going to be doing?"

"Liz knows someone in the United States Dressage Federation who is interested in promoting me as a member of the U.S. Equestrian Team as a dressage competitor and he and the Federation have convinced a wealthy sponsor to buy an international class dressage horse for me. For the sponsor, the horse is a potentially lucrative investment, so he's looking for a stallion that's known to have good breeding potential. They've located a stallion in Germany that fits the bill, so I'm flying to Germany with Liz and the sponsor's sister to see the horse and test ride him."

"Wow, Jess! This is huge for you. I know this will work out for you, Sis. Liz keeps saying you're the most talented rider she's trained in years, and you did great things with Callie."

"I hope so. I'm really nervous, though. I'm hoping Liz does most of the talking. She's used to dealing with people at the highest levels of international dressage. I am not."

"You'll be fine. Just be yourself. You're a great rider and the smartest, kindest person I know. On top of that, you're beautiful. Those people won't have any choice but to like you." She grinned at Jess, but Jessica just rolled her eyes.

Jessica knew her sister was being kind, but she could agree that she was reasonably intelligent and always tried to be nice to people, but there was no way she could be considered beautiful. That was a bit too much. As she passed the mirror in the entryway, she paused to look at her reflection. Looking back was a 5-foot 10-inch tall, slim, twenty-six-year-old woman with shoulder-length brown hair pulled back into a ponytail, bright green eyes, gently arched brows, and a nose that, if you asked her, was just a little too big for her face. She had very few curves, and was probably more muscular than most women due to the fact that she spent her days riding horses. She admitted to herself that she was considered attractive by the guys she went to high school with, but that was long ago, before the accident that changed their lives forever.

As Jessica looked once again at her luggage sitting by the door, the fact that she was traveling thousands of miles and several hours away hit home. "Hailey, are you sure you'll be all right by yourself for the week I'm gone? I'll be so far away, and if anything happens, you'll be on your own without anyone here to help."

Hailey looked heavenward and heaved an exaggerated sigh. "I promise I'll call you every day to check in and let you how I'm doing, and you've already arranged for Mrs. Turner to look in on me too. You have nothing to worry about."

"I want your therapists to call me and update me on your progress as well," Jessica reminded her. "If they don't call me regularly, I'll call them, and I won't give up unless I can speak with them directly. Tell them that, please."

"I will," Hailey promised.

Just then, a car horn sounded in the driveway, and Hailey carefully maneuvered her wheelchair through the narrow front door, down their homemade wooden ramp, and into the driveway. Her friend, Debbie, got out, helped Hailey into the car, then folded her wheelchair and placed it in the trunk of her car. Both girls waved to Jessica as they backed out of the driveway and proceeded on to school.

Jessica sighed to herself. One thing down, now to get dressed and wait for Liz to arrive.

Chapter 4

This is all so surreal, Jessica thought as she scanned the interior of the private Lear jet taking Jessica and her dressage trainer, Elizabeth Randall, to Germany. They were accompanied by Charlotte McMillan, the sister of the wealthy hedge-fund manager, Blake McMillan, the man the USDF had recruited to be Jessica's sponsor. The Lear jet was his as was the limousine that had picked Liz and then Jessica up and brought them to the airport. One of Blake's employees met them on the tarmac and loaded their luggage on the plane, while Jessica and Liz met Charlotte, who had been waiting for them. The trip had been planned just last week, when Jessica and Elizabeth had met Blake and Charlotte at the offices of the USDF and Blake had agreed to sponsor Jessica and purchase an internationally competitive horse for her so that she could pursue her dream of representing her country at the Dressage World Cup next year.

Jessica thought back to the meeting at the USDF offices in Lexington, Kentucky where she and Liz met Blake and Charlotte McMillan for the first time. When the USDF told Liz that they had found her a wealthy sponsor, Jessica had pictured an older, distinguished businessman, probably in his 60's with gray hair and a paunch. Blake McMillan was nothing like what she expected. He was in his mid-30's with perfectly coiffed blonde hair, a body that could only have been built by regular workouts, and a suit that probably cost more than her entire wardrobe. He wore an expression of haughty disdain that declared that he was accustomed to getting what he wanted. He smiled at Jessica during their meeting, and it was clear to her that he considered himself God's gift to women and expected her to melt at his brilliant smile and perfect appearance. When he asked her questions about her ambitions in dressage and her hopes for the future, Jessica noted there was something about Blake McMillan that left her feeling cold. His eyes were a clear, pale gray, and they seemed to look at her as if she were a possession, not a person. She inwardly shivered at the lack of warmth, and vowed not to be alone in a room with Blake. This man was dangerous.

On those thoughts, Jessica mentally shook herself and brought her focus back to the present. As she took her seat across from Liz and Charlotte and buckled herself in, Jessica looked out of her window and couldn't help the wave of uncertainty and apprehension that threatened to overwhelm her. She grasped the armrests on either side of her seat and took a deep breath. As she exhaled and her nerves steadied, Jessica turned to face Liz and Charlotte and smiled self-consciously. The two women had to have noticed that she was not completely comfortable in this opulent environment. Truth be told, this was only the second time in her twenty-six years she had even been on an airplane. She closed her eyes and relaxed back into the plush leather seat, letting her mind wander as the flight crew completed their preparations for take-off.

Once the jet reached a comfortable cruising altitude, a beautiful female flight attendant approached the women and asked them if they'd like a drink, or something to eat while they waited. Charlotte, who had probably traveled the world in this jet working for her brother, ordered champagne for everyone. After it was served in beautifully crafted crystal flutes, accompanied by bite-sized sandwiches and various hors d'oeuvres, the women relaxed and toasted Jessica's future and anticipated success with the stallion Tempest. It wasn't long before the Captain came on the intercom and informed them they had about 6 hours of flight time to Germany.

What would her parents think about all this? Her mother had especially encouraged her to follow her love of horses and to pursue riding as a hobby from the time she was in junior high. She convinced Jessica's father to buy Jessica her first horse, and even helped her to find Liz, a dressage trainer with international competitive experience, who recognized Jessica's talent and ease with horses immediately. By high school Jessica had outgrown her first horse, and Liz suggested Jessica ride Liz's former competition horse, Calliope, nicknamed Callie. The two bonded famously, and won many competitions at the regional and national level.

Jessica's mother had been there all along the way, acting as part-time groom, stall cleaner, hair dresser and chauffeur, always there with an encouraging word, a smile, a hug, or whatever Jessica needed to ensure the best possible performance, but now she was gone, taken away suddenly in the accident that had also killed her father and permanently maimed Hailey.

Jessica missed her terribly. She remembered that day as if it were yesterday. She and Liz were returning from a weekend horse show when Jessica's cell phone rang with a call from the Ohio State Highway Patrol informing her that her parents and sister had been in an accident, her parents had died at the scene, and Hailey had been rushed to the hospital. From there, things only got worse, especially when she was told what the cause of the single car accident was. Her father had been driving drunk, and lost control of the car, sending it over an embankment. In one disastrous moment, Jessica's life had changed irrevocably. Her heart constricted and she closed her eyes as they grew moist with tears, and tried valiantly to bring herself back to the present. When she was certain she had her emotions back under control, she opened her eyes.

Jessica's eyes met Liz's, and Liz noticed Jessica's sorrowful expression. "Is everything okay, Jess?" She asked.

"I'm fine, just daydreaming," Jessica replied. She forced herself to smile reassuringly at Liz, who smiled back with warmth, and, Jessica thought gratefully, encouragement. Liz had been a godsend to Jessica since the accident, and had supported Jessica in many ways. It suddenly became clear to Jessica that it wasn't just Hailey she was doing this for, but Liz. She owed Liz so much, and now that Jessica was in a position to help her, she had to go on.

Now Jessica, Liz, and Blake's sister Charlotte were flying to Hamburg, Germany, to test ride the brilliant, but according to rumors, troublesome stallion, Tempest, owned by the German breeder August Mendelssohn. Charlotte McMillan was a beautiful woman in her mid-30's dressed in the height of fashion, and to Jessica and Liz's delight, was an amateur dressage rider herself.

Unlike her brother Blake, Charlotte was warm and friendly, and Jessica liked her immediately. Charlotte admitted that she accompanied them not just to act as Blake's representative to ensure they were in direct contact with Blake for negotiations with the stallion's owner, but also out of curiosity about the stallion they were traveling to see. Charlotte also related that immediately prior to boarding the jet, Blake called to let her know Mendelssohn had informed him there was another potential buyer in the picture, and that Blake wanted Charlotte to reassure Jessica that all of his resources were available to put toward the effort to get Tempest for Jessica. The identity of the third party was still a mystery, and the potential that their plans could come to naught had them all much more nervous than they would have otherwise been.

The women spent the several hours of the flight getting to know each other better, and Jessica started to relax and enjoy the time away from her many responsibilities at home. Charlotte, she learned, was a dedicated amateur dressage rider who occasionally competed at the Prix St. George level on a beautiful Danish Warmblood gelding with the rather intimidating registered name Matador's Sword. Charlotte laughed as she explained that "Mattie" was gentle as a kitten, and very spoiled. As Charlotte showed Jessica and Liz some cell phone video of her riding Mattie at a recent horse show, Jessica had to admit the two made a compelling pair. Trainer to the core, Liz had offered Charlotte some advice when she indicated there were some trouble spots in the test, and Charlotte understood and expressed her appreciation for the advice.

The conversation turned to the reason for their trip. "I'm really looking forward to seeing this stallion in person," Charlotte said. "I've heard so much about him, and his video was very impressive."

"Yes," Liz said. "I'm looking forward to watching Jessica ride him. From what I've seen in the video, and what I know of this horse's breeding, I think they'll be a great fit."

"I understand from the USDF that the German rider, Hermann Wolfe, was getting disappointing results from Tempest, and that Mendelssohn himself took the stallion away from Wolfe."

Jessica wasn't certain she should believe the rumors, but the thought that an international class rider had been having trouble riding Tempest did not help calm her nerves. Nevertheless, she couldn't help being excited about the prospect of having this horse to ride in competition as she looked at the women sitting across from her, "Charlotte, did Blake happen to mention how much Mendelssohn is asking for Tempest?"

"He did say one million dollars, but I don't know how firm that number is. Blake has given me permission to negotiate on his behalf, and has also instructed me to call him if Mendelssohn tries to raise the price above a million. As I told you before we left, Blake said that Mendelssohn told him there was another party interested in the stallion, and that he would be at the farm at the same time we are. If true, it's obviously a blatant attempt by Mendelssohn to encourage a bidding war between two prospective buyers. Not an unheard of practice, but not very professional, if you ask me."

"Did he happen to say who this other prospective buyer is?" Liz asked.

"No. But it's someone he seems to be taking very seriously according to Blake." Charlotte turned to Jessica. "Don't worry Jessica, Blake is committed to buying this stallion. He won't let anyone outbid him on Tempest."

"Well, if I wasn't nervous before, I certainly am now. This is serious business. I have never in my life been near a horse, much less been on a horse, worth a million dollars."

"I don't know, Jess," Liz responded. "Callie is an international class mare, and although I didn't pay that much for her, at one time she could have commanded that kind of price."

"You're right, Liz. I sometimes forget how lucky I am to have a chance to ride such a talented and special horse as Callie. Thank you so much for trusting me with her."

Liz smiled. "I wouldn't have allowed you anywhere near Callie if I thought you couldn't handle her or treat her kindly, Jess. You must know that."

Jessica blushed at the praise implied in Liz's statement. "I suppose that's true Liz, but the amount of trust you've shown me these past few years humbles me. Callie is really a special horse."

Liz nodded in agreement. "She definitely is, but without you, she would never have been able to fulfill her potential. I can't help but think your appearance at my farm was divine intervention. Callie was not happy when I decided to retire her from competition before she was really ready. I'm so glad the two of you found such success before she was injured."

"Well," Charlotte interrupted, "I hate to stop this love fest, but I'd like to get some sleep before we land. I recommend you do the same. You want to be sharp and not jet-lagged when we go to meet your next horse." The women laughed together and settled in to sleep for a few hours before they arrived in Germany.

It wasn't long before the pilot woke them with the announcement that the jet was preparing for landing. Blake had arranged for a car and driver to pick up the trio at the airport, and after they made their way through Customs, they were on their way to the Mendelssohn farm in a stylish black Range Rover. After having talked for most of the plane ride over, and even after a few hours of sleep probably suffering from more than a bit of jet-lag as well after a six-hour flight, the women stayed mostly silent as they drove through the German countryside to the farm just a twenty-minute drive from Hamburg.

Jessica's first thoughts were of Hailey, and she checked her cell phone to make sure Hailey hadn't tried to call her while they were in the air. She had not, but that didn't prevent Jessica from wondering how Hailey was doing on her own. This was the first time since the accident 5 years ago that Jessica had left Hailey alone for more than a day or two. Jessica couldn't help but be worried about her, even if her mind told her there was really nothing to be concerned about.

Jessica's thoughts were interrupted as Charlotte said from the front seat, "Jess, Liz, look. There's the Mendelssohn Farm."

Jessica looked back out the window and saw the large, painted wood sign with the Mendelssohn name and horse head symbol carved boldly in relief, and as their driver took them down the driveway, a group of stables and other outbuildings all formed of a beautifully aged red brick with taupe painted wood shutters appeared. The entrances to each building were arched and nearly two stories tall, offering a look inside that revealed wide brick aisles with polished wood stall doors and decorative iron hardware. All of the buildings were constructed in matching architectural style, and the stables appeared spotless, not a speck of dust or dirt was visible inside. The exterior was also immaculate and the landscaping was artfully and professionally done.

In the distance, Jessica noticed an outdoor riding arena, and in it someone was riding the most spectacular horse she had ever seen. Without a doubt, this horse had to be Tempest. He was at least seventeen hands tall, solid black, with no white markings on his body at all. His body was perfectly proportioned, with a nicely crested neck and powerfully built hindquarters. He moved smoothly, powerfully and effortlessly for the man riding him, and the pair performed as though they had been training together for months, if not years. This must be Mendelssohn's trainer, she thought.

She noticed there were two men watching the pair perform. One of the men was clearly Mendelssohn, an older man with salt and pepper hair, dressed in a tweed wool jacket and corduroy slacks, and wearing a brown plaid driving cap. He was a bit short and stocky but held himself proudly as the owner of the magnificent beast performing for them. The other man was younger, taller, and wore riding boots and breeches. This must be the other potential buyer, Jessica thought. As their car approached the outdoor arena parking area, the men looking on turned to see who had just arrived. Mendelssohn smiled in welcome. The other man kept his face impassive and looked at the women without a hint of a smile. Clearly they were not welcome as far as that gentleman was concerned.

"Greetings, ladies, and welcome to Mendelssohn Farm." Herr Mendelssohn smiled broadly and shook each of their hands. "May I introduce Mr. Lionel Hayes?" Lionel smiled and shook each ladies' hand as well, but the smile was blatantly insincere, a fact they all instantly noticed. "And you may recognize the gentleman riding Tempest. He is, of course, Mr. Michael Stafford."

Jessica couldn't stop the gasp that escaped her lips as her attention immediately fixed on the man astride the magnificent black stallion. Of course, they all knew who Michael Stafford was. He had won team and individual gold medals at last summer's Olympic Games riding the incredible Danish Warmblood stallion, Romeo. The pair was famous, and had scored the highest marks in international dressage competition anyone had ever seen, setting a new World Record in their Grand Prix Special test which served to elevate the British team to the gold medal. Everyone expected the pair to dominate international competition for the foreseeable future, until suddenly and unexpectedly, Romeo's owners reclaimed the stallion and took him out of competition so that they could capitalize on his fame by offering him up for stud.

The dressage community was shocked by the owners' blatant abandonment of Michael, but ultimately had to acknowledge that the stallion's owners, having invested as much money as they had in the horse, had every right to do with him as they pleased.

Michael, from all accounts, was devastated by the loss of his mount, and had yet to find a new horse to compete internationally. Rumor also had it that Michael's sudden exit from the international spotlight triggered the loss of his fiancée as well, which in turn had triggered a great deal of bad behavior fueled by excessive drinking.

As she watched from just outside the fence, Jessica couldn't help but admire the way Michael masterfully controlled the obviously powerful and, if rumors were correct, willful stallion with apparent ease. As Michael rode Tempest through a relaxed passage into a perfectly executed piaffe, then back to passage with clear transitions between the movements, Jessica's attention moved from the pair as a unit to Michael himself. He had long, muscular legs that hugged Tempest's body perfectly, and his position on the horse was classically perfect.

Even though he was wearing a jacket, Jessica could see he had broad shoulders, and muscular arms. She could also see that his long, gloved fingers were lightly playing with Tempest's mouth through the reins and double bridle, and the sensitivity he displayed in that moment took Jessica's breath away. His face was partially hidden by his safety helmet, but she could see that he was completely focused on the horse he was riding, his square jaw looking set, and she could see his lips moving slightly, as if he were talking quietly to Tempest as he rode him. She could also see the stallion responding to his voice and touch, as his ears flicked back and forth several times as they moved around the arena. The softness she could see in Michael's expression and the slight smile on his face instantly communicated to Jessica that Michael was clearly enjoying himself as he put Tempest through his paces.

Jessica had never seen such an instant rapport between a human being and horse, and she was awed by the experience.

Michael's attention was focused entirely on the horse he was riding, and only marginally noticed the three women that had just arrived and who were watching him with open admiration. He could also tell that Tempest realized he had a new audience. His energy level increased just a bit, and his neck arched in a blatant display of masculine pride. He puffed himself up and snorted briefly and loudly to ensure he had everyone's attention. "So, old man, you see you have a new audience to perform for," Michael said softly, "I don't blame you for wanting to show off a bit for the ladies, but do me a favor, and behave yourself. Take my word for it, ladies don't appreciate rudeness in their males, no matter the persuasion."

The stallion seemed to understand Michael's words, because he instantly settled into a relaxed and powerful canter, as Michael guided him to execute a perfect canter pirouette before moving easily into a canter half pass followed by an effortless flying lead change at the rail. "Well done, boy. Splendid!" Michael smiled and praised Tempest, gave him a brief pat on the neck just above the withers, and reluctantly transitioned back to walk, allowing Tempest to have a long rein and stretch. He noticed there was a groom waiting to finish cooling the stallion out, so he halted and proceeded to dismount. As he ran up the stirrup leathers, he steeled himself to meet the three women who had just arrived. He reminded himself that these women were the competition, and he selfishly hoped they had observed how well he and Tempest had fit. He knew after having ridden this horse that he had to have Tempest for his own.

Before returning Tempest to the groom, Michael took a few moments to stroke Tempest's powerful neck, rub his withers, and murmur his thanks to the stallion for being on his best behavior. He handed Tempest's reins to the groom and turned to approach the group at the fence. "Herr Mendelssohn, you have my compliments. Tempest is a magnificent animal."

"Many thanks, Mr. Stafford," Mendelssohn replied, "It's clear you have a rapport with the horse that I have seldom seen in my experience."

"I have to agree," Liz said, "Mr. Stafford, you rode the horse masterfully."

Michael turned his attention to the woman. "Thank you, Miss . . .?"

Mendelssohn noticed the hesitation and realized that Michael had not yet been introduced to his audience. He quickly moved to introduce the women. "Michael Stafford, I'd like you to meet Mrs. Elizabeth Randall, Miss Charlotte McMillan, and Miss Jessica Warren." It was Elizabeth Randall who had spoken to him, but as he was introduced to each of the women, his attention was drawn not to the fashionably dressed woman standing immediately to Mrs. Randall's left, but to the tall young woman standing next to her.

Miss Jessica Warren was an attractive mahogany brunette in her mid-to-late 20's he guessed, with skin tanned a golden brown by many hours outdoors, and a slim, but not too slim figure. She had a long, straight nose, and square, but delicate chin. It was her eyes, though, that caught and held his attention. They were bright green with gold and brown flecks under perfectly arched brows, but what struck him most about them was not only the intelligence, but the maturity they reflected. Miss Warren's eyes reflected a wisdom not often seen in women her age and, if he wasn't mistaken, a hint of sadness as well. He also noticed small worry lines gracing her brow not normally present on the faces of women her age. He found himself wondering what the source of her worries might be, and whether he might be able to relieve her of whatever burden she was carrying. Surprised at the direction his thoughts had taken, Michael quickly shifted his gaze from Jessica to address Liz directly.

"Thank you, Mrs. Randall. Coming from you that is high praise, indeed." He had heard of Elizabeth Randall, and knew that she was a well-respected American dressage rider and trainer with a great deal of experience competing on the international stage, and knew at that moment that this competition was going to be serious. "As you probably know, I'm no longer riding Romeo, and am looking for a new mount. Tempest is a magnificent animal, and Herr Mendelssohn was kind enough to allow me an opportunity to try him out."

"We're also here at Herr Mendelssohn's invitation to try Tempest out," Liz replied. "Jessica needs a mount capable of competing at the World Cup next year, and possibly the Olympics three years from now. Tempest is one of the few horses in the world available now for sale that has the training and international experience Jessica needs. We're serious about purchasing him. Herr Mendelssohn has agreed to allow Jessica to ride Tempest tomorrow before any decisions are made about his future."

"If Herr Mendelssohn has agreed," Michael said. "I have no problem with that."

Jessica felt the tension between Liz and Michael Stafford, and looked at Charlotte for guidance. Her eyebrows lifted in question. *What's going on here? Should I be worried?* Charlotte almost imperceptibly shook her head to indicate no. Nothing to worry about.

"Of course, of course," Mendelssohn interjected in an attempt to defuse tension. "I had always intended for both of you to ride Tempest before any decisions are made about his future. Miss Warren will ride him tomorrow."

During the somewhat tense interaction between Michael and Liz, Jessica made some judgments of her own about Michael Stafford. Jessica could clearly see that the photos she had seen of him in the magazines didn't do him justice. If anything, he was even more handsome in person than he was in the magazines. His clear, cobalt blue eyes seemed to look right through her, and contrasted strikingly with his thick, wavy jet-black hair. He was tall, probably about six feet, two inches, and athletically built.

He spoke with a distinctly British accent in a smooth baritone voice and when she heard it Jessica understood at least in part how Michael was able to work so well with horses. The velvet tone of that deep baritone voice calmed her and instantly made her feel comfortable in his presence. The timbre of his voice resonated within her. She had never experienced such an overwhelming sensation of peace as she listened to Michael converse with Liz and explain how he had been putting Tempest through his paces. *I'll never have a chance,* Jess thought to herself.

Lionel was taken aback. Neither he nor Michael had been told that there would be competition for Tempest. This changed Lionel's thinking drastically. Roberta's diligence in finding Tempest for Michael had thrown Lionel's plans awry, and had succeeded in giving Michael hope. There was no way he could prevent Michael from taking the opportunity presented to him to have a horse he could take into competition relatively quickly. Now that there was a possibility that Michael might not have Tempest after all, Lionel's hopes raised. Maybe Jessica Warren was exactly the answer to this most recent threat to his plans.

Chapter 5

After arranging a time with Mendelssohn for Jessica to ride Tempest the next day, the three women had their driver take them to a lodging house in Hamburg that Mendelssohn had recommended. After checking in, and agreeing to meet in 30 minutes for dinner, they each made their way to their assigned rooms and settled in. Jessica showered and changed into dress slacks and a lightweight sweater, and returned to the Inn's dining area.

Liz and Charlotte were waiting for her at a table, and she approached them and took the empty seat.

"Well, Jess, what do you think of your competition?" Charlotte asked.

"Are you kidding me?" Jessica responded. "Michael Stafford is one of the best dressage riders in the world. How can I ever compete against him?" Jessica felt overwhelmed with this most recent turn of events. In just a matter of hours, her feelings of excitement and anticipation turned to anxiety and discouragement.

"This isn't over, Jess," Liz said. "I know Michael Stafford is a great rider, but he hasn't ridden an international class horse in nearly a year. In fact, he hasn't even competed for quite some time," Liz continued. "On top of that, rumor has it that he doesn't have the funds to purchase Tempest. If that's the case, he has to convince Mendelssohn to sponsor him. We, on the other hand, have the funds to purchase Tempest and can assure Mendelssohn that with your USET backing, there's a near certainty that he will compete on the international stage within months after the purchase. I don't think Michael can make that promise. All is not lost."

Jessica looked skeptically at Liz. "I watched him ride today, Liz, and you did too. Did you see anything that makes you think he's in any way rusty? He was magnificent, and Tempest was putty in his hands. I've never seen anything like it, and he was riding the horse for the first time."

"I admit that he's a very talented rider, Jess, but you're a brilliant rider in your own right, and I'll be right there with you tomorrow. You can do this."

"If you say so, Liz, I have to believe you. I'm not giving up." Jessica sighed and perused the menu then placed her order with the waitress serving their table. She turned to Liz. "I'm counting on you to keep me grounded tomorrow. There's a good chance Michael and his friend will be there to watch us, and I will be a nervous wreck. If Tempest senses my nerves, he'll react accordingly. I need you to keep me grounded and focused, or I'm not going to perform at my best."

"Absolutely, Jess," Liz said. "Let's start by going over what your plan is for riding Tempest tomorrow."

"I thought it would be best for me get on him first, to take some time to get him warmed up and gauge his reactivity and sensitivity to the aids. That way, I'll be better able to guide you through your ride."

"I like that plan. I was hoping you would agree to ride him first. I've never ridden a stallion before, and any insight you can give me would be priceless."

"Stallions aren't that much different from mares really. You always have to establish you're the leader. With a mare, like Callie, you need to gently lead. With a stallion, you have to be certain to establish your dominance early, or he'll try to take control and bully you. After I've had a chance to ride him, I'll have a better idea how much strength you'll need. I know Michael didn't seem to be working very hard to control Tempest, but he's got long, muscular legs and he's accustomed to riding a stallion, so his ride may not be very helpful to us."

"I just don't want to let you down, Liz," Jessica responded. "I know how much you need the funds we can earn from competing well at the Olympics to rescue your farm from foreclosure."

"Don't worry about me, Jess. If this doesn't work out, I'll figure out some other way to save the farm."

"Not if your soon-to-be ex-husband has anything to say about it. From the way he's been behaving, Rick wants to see your dream destroyed in the worst possible way. Why else would he be so persistent about forcing you to sell the place and pay him off to the tune of a quarter million dollars?"

"I don't want to talk about Rick right now. Let's talk about tomorrow," Liz said, hoping to distract Jessica from this very painful subject, at least for now. The last thing Liz needed was to be reminded about how angry and vindictive her husband had become in past few months. "We have to be as prepared as possible. The best thing we can all do is get some rest. I don't know about you, but I'm feeling some significant jet lag. A good night's sleep is essential if we're going to be at our best tomorrow."

"I agree," Charlotte said. "I'm exhausted. Let's go up to our rooms, get some sleep, and I'll see you both tomorrow morning, bright and early."

The three women, having finished and paid for their meals, made their way back to their rooms. Jessica placed a call to Hailey to check in with her and make sure she was all right. Hailey confirmed that everything was fine, so Jessica changed into her pajamas and settled in for the night.

~ ~ ~

Michael and Lionel had been provided rooms at a guest house on the Mendelssohn farm property, and Mendelssohn had invited his famous guest and his friend to his home for dinner. Although it would have been to his benefit to spend more time with Mendelssohn and press his case for sponsorship, Michael felt as though he needed some time to himself to contemplate the events of the day. He asked Mendelssohn if he could have dinner delivered to his room this evening, and Mendelssohn had agreed. Lionel, on the other hand, decided to take advantage of Mendelssohn's hospitality, and joined him for dinner.

Michael made quick work of the meal Mendelssohn provided—simple but satisfying German fare consisting of whole grain bread, cheese, and deli meat, with mustard and pickles, and a smooth, rich German lager to quench his thirst. He stretched his full length out on the bed in his room. He linked his hands behind his head and looked up at the ceiling, thinking back to his encounter with Miss Jessica Warren, the woman he was competing with for Tempest. Even though he had only just met her, and they had only spoken a few words, Michael knew that she was different from any other woman he had ever encountered.

Since his Olympic success, Michael had met several young, attractive women who clamored for his attention as a dressage trainer, and many times as a sexual partner as well. When he was engaged to Emma, Michael tried as best he could to gently distance himself from encounters with the women he soon came to understand weren't nearly as interested in learning dressage from him, but were more interested in bragging to their friends that they had "hooked up" with the famous and very good-looking Michael Stafford. However, this young woman, although about the same age as many of the "groupies" he had encountered, was different. She was so serious she initially appeared much older than she was.

When he and Lionel had returned to their rooms after his ride, Michael had searched the internet and learned that

Jessica was only 26 years old. He also read a recent profile of her in *Dressage Today* magazine. He learned that Jessica had lost her parents in an automobile accident 5 years ago. The accident had also so severely injured her sister Hailey's legs that they both had to be amputated below the knee. No wonder Jessica carried herself in such a mature way. She had been forced by circumstances to grow up quickly. At the very young age of 21, she had become the legal guardian of her disabled sister, and the sole means of financial support for their small family. His respect for Jessica grew with that knowledge. She was, definitely, a remarkable young woman.

Just from their brief interaction earlier today, Michael sensed that Jessica Warren was not only intelligent and beautiful, but she carried serious burdens no one her age should be carrying. Her face was careworn and her eyes showed a hint of sadness even when she smiled and interacted with her mentor and trainer and the sponsor's sister. Now he knew why. He was surprised to realize that a part of him instinctively wanted to find some way to help her, and bring some happiness to her life. If only he could step aside and allow her to have Tempest for herself. Michael shook himself from his reverie and chuckled to himself. Unfortunately, he needed Tempest and the funds he could earn from showing him, to help Ian. Not to mention the fact that Michael Stafford was the last person to help someone fix their problems. He had way too many of his own.

Chapter 6

Lionel was seated with Mendelssohn for dinner that evening. "Herr Mendelssohn," Lionel said. "Thank you for your wonderful hospitality. I apologize on Michael's behalf that he was not able to join us. He has been through a lot lately, and needed some time to himself."

"Yes, of course, Mr. Hayes," Mendelssohn replied. "I have heard rumors that Mr. Stafford has not been the same since his fiancée left him several months ago."

Lionel could tell that Mendelssohn was bursting with curiosity to see if the rumors about Michael were true. Was he really a hopeless drunkard and womanizer, and had he lost his touch with horses? Obviously, from Michael's remarkable demonstration on Tempest today, he hadn't lost his abilities as a rider, but Lionel was eager to leave Mendelssohn with the impression that Michael couldn't be trusted with a horse as valuable as Tempest – especially now that Michael had viable competition in the guise of the American dressage star, Jessica Warren.

"Well, Herr Mendelssohn," Lionel began, with apparent reluctance, "I really shouldn't be telling you this, but I'm very worried about Michael."

"Why are you worried?" Mendelssohn replied.

"Michael has been, well, different since Emma left him. He's been trying to find solace in alcohol and one-night stands with anonymous women. He has lost several clients and his training yard isn't nearly full. To add insult to injury, his brother was recently charged with manslaughter in connection with a bar fight. I don't think his mind is in his riding at all."

"I see," Mendelssohn said, clearly disturbed by the information Lionel was providing him. "I must say, this concerns me."

"Please, Herr Mendelssohn," Lionel responded, trying as best he could to look concerned, and not to smile, "Michael really needs this opportunity to redeem himself with the dressage world. Your trust in him, despite his recent history, would be invaluable."

"Thank you, Mr. Hayes," Mendelssohn said. "I very much appreciate this information."

"I would appreciate it if you didn't tell Michael I've told you any of this. He would be extremely embarrassed, not to mention angry with me for my candor with you. I've only told you this because I know I can trust your discretion," Lionel said.

"Of course, Mr. Hayes, you have it."

Lionel smiled. He had made a great deal of progress today in ruining Michael's chances to get a sponsorship from Mendelssohn. It was, of course, the least he could do.

~ ~ ~

The next day dawned clear and cool, and Jessica was experiencing the worst nerves of her riding career. She knew in her heart that her success in riding this stallion would make or break her dream of competing in dressage on the international stage, and Jessica could feel the weight of the pressure like nothing she had ever felt before. *All right, Jess, get a hold of yourself and do this. You're good. No, you're better than good, you're one of the best dressage riders in America. Don't let this Brit or this big horse scare you.* She took a deep breath, looked at her reflection in the mirror and saw a pale, but professionally turned-out young woman with a look of determination in her eyes, and knew that she was as ready as she ever would be for the ride of her life.

As Jessica left her room to meet Liz and Charlotte in the lobby of their inn, she remembered that she had left her ever-present cell phone plugged in to charge in the room. She retrieved it and left her room to meet her companions. As she went to the lobby, she checked her phone, and there were no missed calls or text messages. Hailey must be doing all right, or she would certainly have heard from the Turners or Hailey herself. Jessica relaxed a bit. At least that's one thing she wouldn't have to worry about today. As she approached Liz and Charlotte, her nerves reappeared, and in an attempt to chase them away, she took another deep breath and forced what she hoped was a cheery smile on her face.

"Hey, ladies," Jessica said. "How are you both this fine morning?"

"We're fine. More importantly, how are you doing?" Charlotte responded. Not unexpectedly, Charlotte was outfitted in the latest designer fashion. Liz was right beside her in riding attire. Before Jessica could respond to Charlotte, Liz said, "She looks confident and ready for her ride. Am I right, Jess?"

Jessica flashed Liz a look of surprise. The last thing she felt was confident and ready to ride. Liz would know that in a heartbeat. The two had been together long enough. At Jessica's quizzical look, Liz surreptitiously glanced quickly at Charlotte, then back to Jessica. It instantly dawned on Jessica that Liz had seen right away that Jessica was nervous, but she didn't want Charlotte, whose brother was about to spend a million dollars on a horse for her, to know she wasn't completely confident in her ability to ride Tempest no matter what. Jessica nodded her head slightly to Liz to acknowledge she understood, then replied. "Yes, Liz, you're right. I'm ready to go."

"Good," Liz said firmly. "Let's eat something before we go. It would be better for you if you can."

"Great. How about something light, though. Maybe a couple of scrambled eggs and a slice of toast?"

"Works for me," Liz said. "Let's go in and place our orders."

The three women went into the inn's dining area and sat down. Liz ordered eggs as well, and Charlotte ordered a traditional German breakfast of soft-boiled eggs, meat, bread, and cheese. They all had coffee. Jessica's nerves calmed enough that she enjoyed her breakfast, and the women were quickly done and ready to go.

Their driver met them in the parking lot, and they made their way to Mendelssohn Farm. As they drove up to the farm, Jessica could see inside the tastefully decorated and lavishly appointed stable and noticed that Michael and Lionel were already there talking with Herr Mendelssohn while a groom was saddling Tempest. The stallion was fidgeting in the cross ties and appeared agitated, his tail occasionally switching in apparent irritation. However, as she watched, Michael reached over to the stallion and said something to the horse while stroking his neck several times in long, smooth strokes from his poll to his withers. The horse seemed to calm almost immediately, and actually reached his head around and nudged Michael's shoulder as if to thank him for the reassurance. Both Mendelssohn and the groom looked at Michael in amazement. Just at that moment, Herr Mendelssohn noticed the women had arrived. He left the men and started walking in their direction.

"Welcome back, ladies." Mendelssohn turned to address Jessica. "As you can see, Tempest is almost ready for your ride today, Miss Warren."

"Actually, Herr Mendelssohn," Liz said. "I will be riding Tempest first, then Jessica will ride. I hope that plan meets with your approval."

Mendelssohn turned to Liz. "Of course, Mrs. Randall. I have every confidence in your abilities." He looked back at Michael and Lionel, who had followed him out of the stable to greet the three women, then again addressed Liz. "Mr. Stafford and Mr. Hayes are my guests here at the farm, and have asked if they might observe your ride. Do either you or Miss Warren mind them staying?"

"No, not at all. We are happy for the gentlemen to stay." Liz looked confidently over to Jessica. "Aren't we, Jess?"

"Sure," Jessica said, hoping the men couldn't hear the tremulousness in her voice as she responded. She looked directly at Michael. "I'd be honored if you stay."

Michael acknowledged Jessica with a slight smile and a brief nod. Jessica thought she saw a flash of what could have been encouragement in his eyes at that instant, but Michael quickly averted his gaze, and Jessica wasn't completely certain she had seen it.

The groom brought Tempest out, and Liz strapped on her riding helmet, went over to him, took the reins from the groom, and led the stallion to the mounting block just outside the outdoor arena. The women had been discussing on the drive over that the crisp, cool morning would most likely find Tempest fresh and full of nervous energy. They were not disappointed. As Liz took the reins from the groom and led him up to the mounting block, he shied away from the mounting block a step or two, and Liz reprimanded him with her voice and firmly brought the stallion back to the block. Liz knew the stallion had seen this mounting block hundreds of times, and was shying in part to test Liz to see what he could get away with. Properly chastised, Tempest stood quietly this time, and Liz was able to lift herself into the saddle easily.

As Jessica and Charlotte, Michael, Lionel and Mendelssohn watched, Liz started out her ride walking Tempest on a long rein to allow him to loosen his back and legs. After a few minutes of that, Liz started shortening the reins and collecting Tempest for more advanced work. The stallion appeared cooperative as Liz shortened the curb and snaffle reins, but suddenly, the stallion gathered himself and with a loud grunt, leaped into the air, kicking out with his hind legs once he was airborne. He squealed loudly and bucked twice in a straight line toward the middle of the riding arena. While all of the spectators' eyes were riveted on the pair, Liz showed her experience by staying calm, and easily moving with the stallion, maintaining her balance as she eased off a bit on the contact from the reins so that Tempest wouldn't feel trapped.

Once she had the stallion back under control, Liz looked over to the spectators, and heaved an exaggerated sigh, and grinned. "Piece of cake!" she called out.

The group of spectators all laughed at Liz's blatant attempt to diffuse a very tense situation, and the tension that Tempest's explosion had created among the spectators quickly disappeared.

The rest of Liz's ride warming up Tempest went smoothly, and after 10 minutes of work, Liz halted the stallion, dismounted, and led him to the mounting block and motioned Jessica to join her. Jessica, with some significant trepidation, strapped on her own safety helmet, squeezed between the fence rails surrounding the riding arena, and slowly approached the pair.

In a low voice, so the rest of the group couldn't hear, Liz instructed Jess, "Despite what you saw, Jess, he's pretty straightforward. To avoid what I experienced, you have to be careful not to hold him too rigidly with the reins. He has a very sensitive mouth, you need to approach him thinking you have his mouth in your hands. Keep your fingers moving and your wrists soft, you will do fine."

Jessica nodded and stepped into the left stirrup, lifting herself into the saddle. She immediately felt Tempest's strength, as he danced a bit in place, adjusting to her weight in the saddle. It was then she felt her cell phone in her back pocket, and quickly removed it and handed it to Liz. She hadn't turned it off, however, because she wanted to make sure if Hailey called, she would know right away. Her attention turned back to Tempest, and she carefully asked him to move forward. He complied, though his back seemed tense, and his head came up, hollowing his back underneath her.

"Relax your seat, Jess. He's sensing some tension from you," Liz said a bit more loudly.

Jessica immediately eased her grip on the reins, and loosened her hip and lower back muscles so her seat could better follow Tempest's movement, and the stallion visibly relaxed and rounded into the contact. From that moment, Jessica relaxed, and easily blocked out the spectators, and everything else outside of the horse beneath her and Liz's voice providing occasional instruction. Thankfully, Liz stayed quiet for the most part, allowing Jessica to find her own way with the magnificent animal she was riding. And he was magnificent. Powerful, ground-eating strides carried her through the trot and canter portions of a mini Grand Prix Special test, which Jessica and Liz had decided they would use to gauge Tempest's readiness to compete at the Grand Prix level.

Michael watched Jessica's ride with rapt attention. As he had suspected, she was a talented rider, with a natural feel for the horse, soft, steady hands and a balanced seat that moved with the horse easily. The picture the pair presented was most impressive. Michael listened as Elizabeth offered occasional guidance as Jessica rode through the test, but mainly he and the other spectators watched in admiration as Jessica handled the stallion with relative ease. To his surprise, Michael found himself wishing he and Jessica were not competing against each other for this horse. For the first time since Emma left him, he found himself desiring another woman for more than just a one-night stand. This woman was different in so many ways from any other woman he had encountered. He was definitely intrigued.

When Jessica trusted Tempest enough to give him a long rein and see how his extended walk looked and felt, she was ecstatic. She could do this. Her confidence soared. Since her ride had been so successful, Jessica relaxed in the saddle and allowed her thoughts to drift to Hailey, and how she was doing back home. Jessica had tried several times to reach her doctors, then her physical therapists without success, and she was frustrated because she was concerned that Hailey's poor-quality prosthetics were getting in the way of her progress.

Tempest, who had started getting bored at the lack of challenging work in the past few minutes, noticed right away that Jessica's attention was no longer on him. His focus strayed to the activity outside the arena, looking for anything of interest that might occupy his mind, and possibly give him an opportunity to assert himself to test this new rider's resolve. At that moment, Jessica's cell phone, which Liz had placed on one of the fence posts surrounding the riding arena, rang loudly. Tempest, knowing instinctively at that moment that he had the upper hand, reacted more dramatically to the sudden sound of the cell phone than would have been expected, and suddenly, without warning, he violently dove his head between his knees, at the same time throwing a powerful buck. Then he immediately spun and bolted away from the noise.

Jessica was taken completely by surprise, as were the observers. Liz, seeing that Jessica was in some trouble tried to intervene. "Take it easy, Jess!" Liz shouted. "Shorten the reins, gradually!"

Jessica really tried to do what Liz had instructed, but she apparently had shortened the reins too quickly, because Tempest suddenly stopped and reared to avoid the tension in his mouth, and Jessica was too off balance to remain in the saddle. She pitched off of Tempest's back and hit the ground hard, her hips and low back hit first, her helmeted head whiplashing back and striking the ground soon thereafter.

The spectators all rushed to her aid, Liz and Michael getting there first, while Mendelssohn and his groom were catching and calming Tempest.

"Are you all right?" both Michael and Liz asked simultaneously.

Jessica did a quick inventory of her body, and felt nothing broken, but her hips and back ached, and she had a dull ache in her head.

"I'm fine, I think," she responded. "My pride has taken the biggest hit, along with my butt," she said and blushed with embarrassment.

"Take your time, and let us know when you're ready to get up," Michael said. "We can help you if necessary."

"Thanks," Jessica said, taking a tentatively deep breath to test the integrity of her ribs. "I think I can get up now."

Liz took her left arm and Michael took her right, and she slowly lifted herself to standing. Jessica was more than a little embarrassed and gently disengaged her arms from Liz and Michael, brushed herself off, and made her way gingerly to Mendelssohn and Tempest.

"I'm sorry, Herr Mendelssohn. Is Tempest all right?" Jessica asked.

"He is fine, Miss Warren," Mendelssohn assured her. "Are you all right? That was quite a spill."

"I'm fine. A little bruised, but there's nothing broken as far as I can tell," Jessica said. Then, in a worried voice, she added, "I hope this doesn't disqualify me from contention for Tempest."

"Of course not," Mendelssohn responded. "I must say that I am surprised that Tempest reacted that way to the sound of a cell phone. He isn't normally that sensitive."

Liz smiled. "Herr Mendelssohn, I think Tempest had gotten bored with the rather routine work we asked of him today, and when Jessica gave him a long rein, he decided to take the opportunity the cell phone ring gave him to test her. It doesn't surprise me at all that a sensitive and intelligent stallion would behave in such a way with an unfamiliar rider."

Michael smiled. "I think you're right, Mrs. Randall. My former mount, Romeo, would act up that way occasionally as well – especially if I allowed my mind to wander during our work. I learned to never lose my focus when riding him."

Lionel had watched Jessica's ride with interest. He had been encouraged with the talent Jessica had shown with Tempest, but her lack of control at the end of her ride concerned him. He needed her to be Mendelssohn's choice for Tempest. Michael could not succeed. It was clear that Lionel needed an alternative plan should Jessica not be good enough for Tempest, and Mendelssohn elected to sponsor Michael after all.

Chapter 7

August Mendelssohn had been in the business of breeding warmblood sport horses for nearly thirty years. He knew that producing a horse with the confirmation, gaits, and temperament for international competition in dressage might happen once in a lifetime. Tempest was just such a horse.

That being said, Mendelssohn also knew that the horse was only a part of the total equation. If the perfect horse was paired with an incompetent, insensitive or ignorant rider, that horse's chance to achieve greatness was almost nil. It was the perfect communication and harmony between horse and rider that created champions. That was the primary reason Mendelssohn had ended his sponsorship of the German rider Hermann Wolfe. The man was completely at odds with Tempest, and hadn't a clue how to ride the stallion with the sensitivity he required. What disturbed Mendelssohn most in hindsight about the experience with Wolfe was that when Wolfe test rode Tempest for Mendelssohn, he rode the horse very well. There was no hint of the problems the pair later developed. True, Tempest was hotter than the majority of horses in international competition this week, but Mendelssohn was certain that he could be ridden in competition, and ridden well, by the right rider.

Having now come to that conclusion, Mendelssohn was frustrated. Today, not just one, but three dressage professionals had ridden Tempest very well, but it was just one ride. Thus, his dilemma. His past experience told him that one ride wasn't enough to determine which rider would be best for Tempest for the long term. His experience with Wolfe had proved that to him. Mendelssohn had assumed that Michael Stafford, the clear favorite in his mind because of his Olympic success, would be the best match for a horse like Tempest, but Stafford had come straight out and told him he didn't have the funds, or the backing of a wealthy sponsor recruited by the British Equestrian Team, and therefore couldn't purchase Tempest for the amount Mendelssohn was asking: $1 million. Instead, he wanted Mendelssohn to sponsor him. Not to mention the added difficulties Michael's questionable mental and emotional stability added to the equation. He was grateful, but somewhat troubled that Lionel Hayes had detailed Michael's difficulties to him in confidence over dinner just last night. If Lionel was so worried about Michael that he was willing to share his concerns with a near stranger, his problems must be serious.

On the other hand, he considered Elizabeth Randall and Jessica Warren. Elizabeth, clearly the experienced professional, also rode Tempest well, almost as well as Michael had. Jessica, under Elizabeth's supervision, also rode Tempest competently, but her approach was more tentative. Tempest took advantage of that lack of confidence by unseating her. Given the circumstances, however, the stallion's testing of a new rider was understandable, and Jessica's failure to maintain her seat was also understandable. Mendelssohn didn't hold that against her. Her mental state, specifically a lack of confidence, however, did concern him.

With both of the competitors for Tempest capable of riding him, Mendelssohn was left with the one significant difference between the two: the American rider was backed by an influential trainer and the U.S. Equestrian Team with a sponsor able to transfer $1 million into Mendelssohn's bank account in a matter of days. Those funds would provide a very comfortable retirement for himself and his wife for the rest of their lives. If money were his only motivation,

Mendelssohn's decision would be easy, but he felt a tremendous amount of responsibility for his magnificent stallion. Was he willing to trust his once-in-a-lifetime horse to someone who had money, but had proven herself to be comparably inexperienced and lacked confidence on the international stage, especially when compared with Michael Stafford who had that experience, proven success and an uncanny rapport with the horse?

Mendelssohn sighed. He had invited all of his guests for dinner this evening. They would expect him to make a decision between them. As he mulled over the possibilities in his mind, weighing the two alternatives, knowing that the future of his prize stallion would rest on this decision, he remained frustrated. No clear choice presented itself.

An intriguing third possibility came to mind. He examined the idea over from various perspectives and yes, it could work. If both parties agreed. The more he thought about it the more convinced he was that this was the only way he would find the right rider for Tempest. Now, to convince the others that he was right when he addressed them after dinner tonight. He was not looking forward to it.

~ ~ ~

While Tempest was being put away following Jessica's ride, Mendelssohn had told Michael and Lionel as well as Jessica, Liz and Charlotte that he would make a decision about Tempest's future and announce his decision at dinner that evening. Dinner would be served at 7:00. The group signaled their agreement, and while Jessica, Liz and Charlotte went back to the Inn to shower and change, Michael and Lionel went back to their room at Mendelssohn's guest house. Michael checked his cell phone and noticed that his mother had tried to call him. He immediately returned her call.

"Michael," his mother said. "I'm so glad you called. I wanted to keep you up to date with what has been happening with Ian. We deposited Ian's bail money with the police yesterday, and they've released him into our custody, but they will not let him leave Surrey. We've set him up in your house and we've promised to stay with him until you return from your trip. He is wearing an ankle bracelet to monitor his location at all times, and he is not permitted to leave your property without the court's permission. Even then, he can only go to certain approved locations, such as his attorney's office."

"How is he, Mum?" Michael asked. "When I saw him last, he had physical injuries and his mental state wasn't much better."

"I'm worried about him, Michael," his mother responded. "He's withdrawn and doesn't say more than two words in response to our questions. He does appear to have gotten medical attention before he left the jail. His ribs are wrapped, and the cuts on his face have been bandaged. A couple of them have stitches. We've offered to drive him to the attorney you retained, but he doesn't want to go without you. Do you have any idea when you will be back?"

"It will be soon, Mum," Michael replied. "The stallion's owner is going to announce his decision tonight. I might be back as early as tomorrow night if things don't go my way."

"I hope things work out for you, Michael," his mother said. "It's time you had something good happen for you. This family certainly needs some good news about now."

"Agreed," Michael said. "I'll call you tomorrow when I have more definite plans."

~ ~ ~

The hour had arrived for the group to gather in Mendelssohn's spacious dining room. Jessica, Liz, and Charlotte arrived just as Michael and Lionel were being seated. Jessica noted right away that the room was decorated in a hunting lodge style, with pine paneled walls upon which were hanging various paintings of horses being ridden or running free. The largest painting was on the wall opposite the entry to the room behind the head of the dining table and portrayed horses ridden by red-coated gentlemen and ladies in 19th-century garb surrounded by hounds clearly preparing for a fox hunt. The table was set with decorative china and silverware, and placed along the center of the table were silver candleholders holding lit taper candles. Jessica glanced over at Liz, and noted that she was equally impressed with the formal atmosphere.

Jessica was glad that she had dressed for the evening. She wore a comfortable, but stylish wrap dress in emerald green that matched the color of her eyes exactly. The dress hugged her figure and fell loosely about her hips ending just above her knees. Around her neck, she wore a simple gold chain that Hailey had given her as a gift last Christmas. Liz and Charlotte had also dressed for the evening. Liz wore a charcoal gray pant suit, and Charlotte work a black sheath dress with very expensive-looking pearls. Jessica noted that Michael and Lionel had also dressed for the evening, Michael in a black suit with a designer-brand tie, and Lionel in a slightly more casual tweed sport coat, open-necked dress shirt and navy slacks.

Jessica couldn't help but notice that Michael looked even more handsome when dressed in a suit and tie, and his striking blue eyes reflected the candlelight, looking luminous, and she felt captured by his gaze. She realized that he had caught her staring at him. She blushed with embarrassment, and dropped her gaze to the floor. When she looked up a couple of seconds later, she noticed Michael was grinning at her, and winked mischievously.

Michael's eyes had instantly been drawn to Jessica as she entered the room with her companions. The dress she wore clung to her slim, athletic but feminine figure, and made her eyes look even more green than they had earlier in the light of day. He also noticed that Jessica was staring at him with admiration—a look he had seen from women many times before—but in Jessica's case, the look wasn't predatory or avaricious, it was instead simply and honestly admiring. When she blushed and looked away at the realization he had caught her staring at him, he found himself charmed and drawn to her lack of pretension and obvious innocence. He rewarded her interest by grinning at her and winking.

As the three women took their seats, Herr Mendelssohn positioned himself at the head of the table, his wife Gerta's place was to his right. Michael sat to Mendelssohn's left and Lionel sat to Michael's left. Liz sat next to Gerta, with Jessica, then Charlotte positioned along that side of the table. Gerta was making several trips to the couple's large kitchen bringing in large steaming platters of chicken, venison, and pork, potatoes, and vegetables. The food smelled delicious, and everyone at the table relaxed a bit and passed the platters around the table, taking what they wanted, and settling in to eat the hearty German meal. In an attempt to further defuse any remaining tension in the room, Mendelssohn addressed a question to Michael.

"Mr. Stafford," Mendelssohn began, "you and Mr. Hayes appear to be very good friends. How long have you known each other?"

Michael looked over at Lionel, who smiled back at him and nodded his assent for Michael to answer the question.

"Well, Herr Mendelssohn," Michael began, "Lionel and I have known each other since we were boys together in Bristol. We came from very different backgrounds, truth be told, but we both shared a love of horses. We met because my Uncle Thomas was a horse trainer at the Bristol race track, and I loved spending time with him after school and on weekends, watching him train the young thoroughbreds. I usually rode my bike to the track right from school on weekdays, because my parents own a restaurant in Bristol, and were both working most days there. I sometimes brought my brother Ian with me, because he was younger, and for a time couldn't be home alone if I wasn't there. Lionel was at the track to avoid an abusive father and a neglectful mother, and through sheer stubbornness and determination became a groom, then an exercise rider there. He worked for my uncle on many occasions, but he also worked for other trainers at the track.

"One day Michael noticed one of the other trainers at the track cursing and berating me for some minor offense, and interceded on my behalf," Lionel said. "He reported the verbal abuse to his uncle, who made it a point to warn the trainer off, and I received much better treatment after that." *At least to all appearances*, Lionel thought to himself. Not all the abuse had stopped, however. Michael hadn't known and Lionel was ashamed to share with him he had also been subjected to sexual abuse by one of the more powerful trainers on the track who threatened him with dismissal if he didn't comply. The scars from that experience were invisible and even more devastating to a thirteen-year-old boy confused about his sexuality.

"I made it a point to look for Lionel every time I visited the track to make sure he was OK, and we spent a lot of time together—when he wasn't busy working—watching my uncle train the race horses. We became close," Michael said. "We've been friends ever since."

Lionel mentally winced at that last remark. They had not been friends the entire time. In fact, Lionel hadn't considered himself Michael's friend for over a year, although he was doing his best to convince Michael he was still his friend. Lionel carefully fixed a pleasant expression on his face.

"Michael's right," Lionel said. "Even after we left our respective homes and pursued differing careers with horses, we kept in touch, and met occasionally at competitions, clinics and the like. My path led to working with off-the-track thoroughbreds to prepare them for a second life as pleasure horses. Michael, on the other hand, found a trainer that recognized his talent for dressage and supported his development, even helping him find his Olympic mount, Romeo."

"Lionel is being too modest," Michael interjected. "His work with thoroughbreds led him to find a world class gelding named Accolade that he campaigned successfully on the international stage. He could have qualified for the Olympics."

"That's enough, Michael," Lionel quickly interrupted Michael before he could complete his thought. "These people aren't interested in the details of my Olympic aspirations."

Michael understood immediately why Lionel had interrupted him. He couldn't blame him for not wanting to discuss the details of the British Olympic trials last year. He quickly changed the subject. "Miss Warren, how did you and Elizabeth meet?"

Jess swallowed past the lump that had instantly appeared in her throat as everyone at the table was now looking at her expectantly. She looked over at Liz, who smiled in encouragement. "Liz and I met when I was in junior high. I was the typical horse crazy teenager and wouldn't quit bugging my parents to get me riding lessons. They finally took me to Liz's farm and introduced themselves and me to her and explained that they couldn't afford to buy me a horse, but were interested in my learning to ride from someone who had the patience and experience to teach me. Liz was definitely that person.

I started with a school horse named Jazz that Liz kept specifically for beginners, and I eventually progressed to the point where I needed my own horse. Liz found a great but affordable intermediate horse for me named Sandy, and I started working for her part time after school and on weekends to earn the money to pay for her board and lessons. I competed with Sandy until I was a sophomore in high school. After I graduated from high school, I became a working student for Liz and it was then that Liz allowed me to ride her former international competition partner, Calliope. Callie and I clicked immediately, and we competed first locally, then nationally. She made me look good, no doubt about it, and she taught me so much. It was riding Callie that kept me sane after the accident that killed my parents. I owe her so much. I was devastated when Callie was injured just a couple of months ago and could no longer compete."

"Jessica is being entirely too modest," Liz said. "She was the answer to my prayers when she offered to ride Callie for me. The mare had been restless, and did not appreciate the fact that I had retired her before she was ready. Callie loved competition, and loved the work involved in FEI level dressage. Jessica is a fantastic rider, and has an equally strong work ethic. The two of them made an unbeatable pair, and after a great deal of success at the shows, the US Equestrian Team took notice."

Jessica flushed at Liz's praise. In her mind, it was truly Callie's talent and experience that had led to their success in competition. She was just the lucky person who was in the right place at the right time to take advantage.

Michael had been listening with undivided attention to Jessica's recounting of her history with horses. He admired her determination, and knew that Elizabeth Randall would not have taken Jessica on as a working student if she didn't think she had the talent and work ethic to succeed at dressage at the international level. Although he had Googled Jessica's name yesterday when he discovered she would be his competition for Tempest, what didn't come through in the articles he had read about her was her passion for dressage and her appreciation for the success she had experienced. She clearly didn't have the ego he had experienced from some riders competing at the international level and he was drawn to her humility and relative innocence.

The evening progressed more quickly now that Herr Mendelssohn's guests were becoming more comfortable with each other, and it wasn't long before dessert had been served, and the last dishes cleared away. Mendelssohn stood up and cleared his throat to get his guests' attention.

"Ladies and gentlemen," Mendelssohn began, "I asked all of you here this evening not only for the purpose of breaking bread with you and getting to know you better, but also to announce my decision with regard to Tempest's future."

"Yes, Herr Mendelssohn, we know why we're here," Lionel said. "So please don't keep us in suspense. What is your decision?"

Mendelssohn again cleared his throat, and looked over at Gerta, who nodded and smiled with encouragement. He had discussed his decision in depth with Gerta. Her future as well as his rested on Tempest's success, and she had agreed wholeheartedly with his decision.

"I learned through recent experience with Herr Wolfe that one ride is not sufficient for me to determine the best rider for Tempest. I have, therefore, decided that I have not seen enough of either Miss Warren or Mr. Stafford with Tempest to make a final decision about his future. I need at least sixty days to observe Tempest being ridden by both of you to make my decision. I believe in that way, Tempest will make the decision for me. Whichever of the two of you makes the best showing at a competition here in Germany with Tempest after sixty days will be his rider for the foreseeable future."

"What?" Lionel shouted.

"You can't be serious!" Charlotte exclaimed simultaneously.

Liz exchanged a glance with Michael, who appeared just as stunned as the others. Jessica was conspicuously silent, so

Liz addressed Mendelssohn directly.

"Herr Mendelssohn, how to you intend to observe both Jess and Michael riding and working with Tempest for sixty days?"

"I had hoped you both could stay here on my property and I could arrange a mutually agreeable schedule for equal time with Tempest," Mendelssohn replied.

Michael's shock at Mendelssohn's declaration turned to anger. "Herr Mendelssohn, I must strenuously object to your terms," Michael said. "Your plan is completely unrealistic for a horse with the talent and experience that Tempest has. Even if you do insist on this course, my personal situation will not allow me to participate. My brother Ian is in trouble, and I must return to England right away. He needs me. There is no way on earth I can stay here in Germany for 60 days. If these are your terms, I must respectfully decline. Thank you for the opportunity." He turned to Lionel. "Let's go, Lionel, we're finished here."

As Michael and Lionel got up and began to leave, Mendelssohn panicked. He had not anticipated this kind of complication to his plan, and quite frankly needed to keep Michael as a possible rider option for Tempest. He sought frantically for a solution that would preserve his ability to allow Tempest to choose the rider most compatible for him. A thought came to him and he smiled and reached out to Michael and Lionel. "Please, Mr. Stafford, maybe there is another way. I understand you have a first class riding and training facility in the UK. Because I have created a much more rigorous process to determine who will ultimately have Tempest, I am willing to be flexible. Would you be willing to keep Tempest at your property and allow Miss Warren, Mrs. Randall and I to stay there for sixty days so that both of you will have equal time?"

Michael hesitated as he pondered Mendelssohn's question. His manor house in Surrey had five bedrooms in addition to his master bedroom, but most of those bedrooms had seldom, if ever, been used. There was furniture there, since he had planned to have weekend long clinics which would require participants to stay at least one or two nights, and had set the house up for that purpose. It had been months, though, since any of those rooms had seen any use. It was possible, though, if he wanted Tempest enough, to take on the extra burden. He sighed. He needed what Tempest could provide for him: a return to prominence in the dressage world he had lost through his own recklessness, and the means to earn enough money to fund Ian's defense. He had to continue.

"Yes, Herr Mendelssohn, I do have sufficient space for the three of you. If Miss Warren and Mrs. Randall agree."

While Michael and Mendelsohn were talking, at the other end of the table, Liz and Jessica had quietly been discussing their options. Both of them had obligations at home that made an extended stay in Europe difficult. Liz was in the middle of a nasty divorce and had a daughter with cerebral palsy who needed daily care and supervision. Not to mention her boarding stable and therapeutic riding school to run. Jessica had Hailey to care for, and didn't feel at all comfortable leaving her alone in Ohio for 60 days. Charlotte joined the conversation, and, after Jessica and Liz had explained their reasons for hesitating over the decision to continue, Charlotte offered to work with the USET and Blake to obtain additional funds to either travel Hailey and Liz's daughter Amy to the UK, or to provide the funds for the women to travel home on weekends or at least as necessary to take care of any personal matters required during their absence.

With Charlotte's assurances, Jessica responded to Michael. "Yes, Mr. Stafford, Herr Mendelssohn, we accept your kind offer."

Michael looked over at Charlotte. "Miss McMillan, will

you be staying as well?"

"Since I'm here mainly to handle a purchase," Charlotte said, "and it appears a purchase will not happen for another sixty days, if ever, I will be returning to the States. Rest assured, sir, that both the USET and my brother will hear about this, and I predict that neither will be happy with this development."

"Noted, Miss McMillan," Mendelssohn said. "But I am standing by my plan." He looked over at Michael. "Mr. Stafford, how soon should I plan to ship Tempest to your facility?"

"Let me call my barn manager and have her start making arrangements. We have mares at our facility, and we will have to segregate Tempest from the mares so they're safe and he isn't tempted to misbehave."

"I understand," Mendelssohn replied. "Although Tempest is very well behaved, it is always better to remove temptation whenever possible."

"I will let you know at breakfast tomorrow," Michael said. "Will that suffice?"

"Certainly. Miss Warren, you, Mrs. Randall, and Ms. McMillan are welcome to breakfast here tomorrow morning as well."

"Thank you, Herr Mendelssohn." She looked at Liz and Charlotte, who nodded in acceptance. "We accept. If you will please excuse us, we have arrangements of our own to make to accommodate this major change in plans. If you'll excuse us?"

Mendelssohn nodded. "Of course. I will see you all tomorrow morning."

Chapter 8

Blake McMillan had just been informed his sister Charlotte was back from Germany. Unfortunately, one of his friends was calling, pushing for information on an upcoming corporate merger. "Damn it, Matt, you know I can't tell you whether the merger is going to happen. That would make me guilty of insider trading, and you know the SEC is always on the lookout for financiers willing to violate securities laws." Blake grinned to himself as he baited his friend Matt Marshall with the fact that he had insider information about the biggest corporate merger in years, the knowledge of which, in the right, or wrong, hands could make the holder several million dollars richer, if they played their cards right. Acting on the information at the wrong time, however, could see both of the Wall Street financiers jailed for insider trading, so Blake was treading carefully.

"Look, Matt, as soon as I think it's safe to tell you, I will. You have my word." Blake tried to placate his friend, and it appeared he was successful. He was preparing to hang up when his sister Charlotte walked into his posh, corner office in the brand-new World Trade Center building.

Blake smiled at Charlotte as he hung up the phone. "Hey, sis! How was your trip to Germany? Do I now own a one-million-dollar dressage horse?"

"Actually, no," Liz responded, clearly incensed. "You would not believe what happened when we got to Mendelssohn's farm. None other than Michael Stafford, an Olympic gold medalist, was there to test ride the horse as well. As you would expect, Stafford rode the horse perfectly.

It looked like he'd been riding the horse for years. Fortunately for us, Stafford can't afford to buy Tempest, so Jessica is still in the running, but Mendelssohn isn't yet sure Jessica, even with Liz's training, can handle him. So, Mendelssohn gave both Stafford and Jessica sixty days to ride and train with Tempest, and he would observe the process. At the end of the sixty days, Jessica and Stafford will each ride Tempest in a rated show in Germany, and whichever rider scores the best with him, will have him." Liz took a deep breath and looked at Blake to gauge his reaction.

"I'm new to all this horse stuff, sis, but it doesn't sound like something that happens every day."

"I'm no expert either, but Liz Randall is, and she assures me that she has never seen a horse owner require prospective buyers to jump through hoops like this. It's unheard of."

"So what can we do?" Blake asked.

"Liz called her friend Will Napier at the USDF, and they're as shocked as we are at this turn of events, but they offered very little advice. It appears that the horse owner has ultimate control over who he sells his horse to, and even if we filed a lawsuit to force a sale, we would have marginal potential for success, then there's the fact that we have to find a German lawyer to file our case there, and it will likely take longer than sixty days to get the case before a judge."

"So, let me get this straight. I won't even have the opportunity to buy this horse for at least another sixty days?" Blake was finally beginning to understand why Charlotte was so angry.

"That's right. The horse is being transported to the UK as we speak, to stay at Stafford's farm, and Jessica and Liz will stay there as well."

"Why Stafford's farm?" Blake queried. "That seems to give him an unfair advantage in this so-called competition."

"That's another part of this whole arrangement that I don't like," Charlotte continued. "Stafford's brother is in trouble with the law, and Stafford needs to stay close to home to monitor him while he's out on bail and to help him in his defense."

"You mean to say that Stafford's brother is a criminal, and that he's living on the farm, where Jessica and Liz will be staying as well?" Blake couldn't believe what he was hearing. Charlotte nodded. "That's outrageous! I want to make sure we're doing everything we can to keep Jessica and Liz safe."

"I plan to go back there and stay with Liz and Jessica to make sure nothing untoward happens while they're there," Charlotte said.

"I know that's what you want, sis, but I really need you here right now. The merger we've been monitoring is nearing completion, and we want to move fast to take advantage of the bump in stock price the merger will trigger. You're my expert on the deal, and have all of the relevant information we need. I can't let you go now."

Charlotte sighed. "Isn't there anyone else that work this deal?"

"I'm sorry, Char, but no. You're my expert. No one else will do."

"All right," Charlotte couldn't prevent the look of reluctance acceptance from showing in her expression. "I'll do my best to keep in touch with Jessica via Skype and hope that will be enough."

"Keep me posted," Blake directed. "I'm very concerned about this situation."

"I will." Charlotte made her way to the door and looked back at Blake. It was clear to her that Blake had more than a passing interest in Jessica. "Jessica has a good head on her shoulders. She won't allow herself to get into a situation she can't handle. Plus, Liz is right there with her. She'll be okay."

Blake nodded and flashed Charlotte what he hoped was a reassuring smile. As the door closed behind her, though, Blake couldn't help but be disturbed by this latest turn of events. He had hoped Jessica would be returning immediately to the States, grateful to him for buying her the horse of dreams. So grateful in fact that she would be amenable to becoming his girlfriend, and soon thereafter his lover. He was so looking forward to showing her off to his friends as his latest conquest.

His mind drifted to a vision of Jessica naked in his bed, her long, shapely legs wrapped tightly around his body as he pounded into her, both of them moaning with pleasure, their hot, sweating bodies moving as one. He felt himself harden, and moved to hide the lower part of his body behind his desk, and adjusted his pants slightly to accommodate his increased size. Bringing himself back to reality, he resigned himself to the fact that his fantasies would not be fulfilled any time soon.

This situation with Stafford's brother concerned him, though. Maybe when things quieted down with the merger, he could fly to the UK personally, and make sure Jessica was all right, and that she realized how much he valued her. Maybe then she would be willing to show her gratitude for his concern. He smiled. Yes, that was an excellent idea.

~ ~ ~

"Please don't worry, Charlotte." Jessica had contacted Charlotte via Skype as Charlotte had insisted she do when they parted at Heathrow airport just a week ago. "Michael has been the perfect gentleman and an excellent host. I barely see his brother, Ian, and when I do, he keeps to himself, and doesn't appear to be dangerous in the least. Liz and I are feeling right at home here, and are impatiently waiting for Tempest to be delivered. We've been told it could be as early as tomorrow."

"So it's Michael now, is it?" Charlotte teased. "You two must be getting along all right to be on a first-name basis so soon."

Jessica felt herself blush, and hoped her computer's camera wasn't sensitive enough to transmit that detail to Charlotte. Of all the information she had just provided her, Charlotte had chosen that particular detail to notice. "Well, we have been living in the same house for nearly a week, and it's just easier to call each other by our first names than be more formal. Michael is very informal anyway, and his manner invites others to be the same way. He isn't at all the man I expected him to be, Charlotte. He's actually really warm and friendly, although he has been keeping Liz and me at arm's length, probably because ultimately, we're the competition trying to take Tempest away from him.

"Away from him? Who says he has him to begin with?" Charlotte responded, feeling a bit irritated that Jessica was already selling herself short by allowing Michael the upper hand in their competition before they even began. Charlotte had been competing against men her entire career, and knew that it could be deadly to Jessica's chances if she gave Michael Stafford even a scintilla of a head start in the competition.

"Charlotte, you know Mendelssohn was impressed with how Michael had ridden Tempest from the very beginning. It was only the fact the Michael didn't have the money to buy him outright that created this competition at all." Even so, Jessica had to acknowledge that she still had hopes that she might have Tempest as her own. Contrary to what Charlotte was intimating, Jessica was determined that she give everything she had to this competition, and give herself a fighting chance to win. "Don't worry, Charlotte, I'm in this competition to win. This won't be easy for Michael. You have my word."

Charlotte smiled. "In that case, I'll sign off and let you prepare. Is all of your equipment there? Do you have everything you and Liz need? You said Tempest is supposed to arrive there tomorrow, right?"

Jessica laughed. "Yes, to all your questions. Everything arrived here in excellent condition, and all is on schedule for Tempest to arrive tomorrow. Now, I have to go. I need to call my sister Hailey and make sure she's okay. Thanks, Charlotte, for everything."

"You're welcome," Charlotte responded. "By the way, Blake sends his regards, and wanted me to let you know he's thinking about you and is concerned for you. I think you've made a conquest of my big brother. I've never seen him so interested in a woman, quite frankly."

Jessica wasn't sure how to respond to that. Blake McMillan was a very rich, handsome man who could have any woman he wanted. What could he possibly see in a horse-crazy, small-town girl from Ohio? "I think you must be mistaken, Charlotte. I can't image what a man like Blake could see in me. I do appreciate the sentiment, though. Please thank him for me, and make sure he knows I am doing well."

"I will," Charlotte said. "I'll call tomorrow, same time. OK?"

"Fine." Jessica smiled and signed off, still puzzled about what Charlotte had told her. Surely, a man as successful, wealthy and accomplished as Blake McMillan wasn't interested in her as more than just a struggling American rider needing financial support. Most likely Charlotte was just ensuring Jessica that Blake wasn't going to abandon her just because their original plans for Tempest had changed. Of course, Jessica nodded to herself, that must be it. There certainly couldn't be any other reason.

Chapter 9

"Take it easy, Michael. You're making me nervous," Tiffany Merchant, Michael's trusted barn manager and friend, had been watching Michael pace up and down the barn aisle for at least 15 minutes before she finally lost patience, and had to say something.

"I'm sorry, Tiff." Michael at least had the courtesy of looking sheepish when he looked at her. "Mendelssohn is arriving with Tempest any time now, and I'm worried he won't think this facility is up to his standards."

Tiffany couldn't believe her ears. She and her staff of three had been working night and day for the past week to adapt the barn and pastures to accommodate a stallion among an established stable of geldings and mares in training. She was proud of the final product, and was extremely aggravated with Michael for his lack of faith in their efforts. "Michael, I don't see anything Mendelssohn could find fault with. This place was already well built and beautiful to look at. Now, it's a model of a modern and efficient equestrian facility."

Secretly, Tiffany hoped that Michael had the money to fund these improvements, but funds had been notoriously short for quite some time. She sighed. Michael's finances were really none of her business. As long as she was paid and had enough money to feed and care for the horses, she should be happy. She was also Michael's friend, however, and she knew about Ian and his problems, and had endured Michael's despair when Emma left so suddenly and unexpectedly. She knew Michael had suffered these past few months, and deserved something good to happen to him. Having Mendelssohn sponsor him with Tempest would be just what he needed to get himself back on his feet. She hoped with all her heart that this worked out for him.

Tiffany had also met Jessica Warren and Liz Randall, and knew that Michael's path would not be easy. Both women were impressive, and she had recognized Liz's name from dressage publications Michael subscribed to and loaned to Tiffany to read. She had Googled Jessica, and learned what she could about her as well. It was clear she was an up and coming young rider with a great deal of talent, who desperately needed a horse if she wanted to continue to compete internationally.

Like Michael, Liz had international dressage experience, and when Tiffany gave her and Jessica a tour of Michael's training yard and introduced her to the horses Michael had in training, Liz asked pertinent questions, and offered some tips for some minor care issues Tiffany had been experiencing. Liz had even asked Tiffany if she thought Michael would allow her to ride one or two of his training horses so she could stay in shape. Privately, Tiffany thought Michael would be thrilled at the prospect, but couldn't make that commitment to Liz, so she told her she would have to ask Michael about that.

Just as they completed their tour, Liz's cell phone rang, and after checking the number, Liz quickly excused herself to take the call. "Hello, Bob, what's up?" Liz knew that her attorney would not be calling her unless some aspect of her divorce proceeding had changed.

"I'm sorry, Liz, but I have bad news. Rick has filed a motion asking the court to grant him full custody of Amy. He's using your extended trip to the UK as evidence that you're unfit to share equal custody."

"No!" Liz's heart sank. "I can't believe it." After recovering from her initial shock, Liz's mind raced to find a solution to her dilemma. First, she had to determine how serious Rick's suit was. "There's no way he can win, Bob, right?"

"Well, Liz, I can't rule out the possibility. This trial period will keep you away from home for over two months, and Amy requires constant care. The temporary situation you've set up with your sister moving into your home isn't ideal, and the fact that the reason you're gone centers on dressage bolster's Rick's allegations that you care more about your career than you do about being a mother."

"I hate to admit it, but you're probably right. This change in plans has put me in a terrible position." Liz sighed deeply. "Is there anything I can do short of abandoning Jessica and coming right back home that will give me a fighting chance to keep custody of Amy?"

"I'm not certain, but I think if you can establish a regular schedule of visits over the two months you're training Jessica, it would help. It would also help to establish that this two-month period is the only time you'll be out of the country, and that you won't be leaving again any time soon," Bob replied.

"I'll speak with Charlotte McMillan right away and make those arrangements. I think I can give Jessica enough to work on during the brief periods I'll be gone to see us through this two months."

"Good. I'll start preparing my response to his motion and request a hearing. I'll send you dates as soon as possible. In the meantime, I recommend you call Amy and tell her what's happening."

"Good idea. She will want to know that her mother and father are fighting again, and why. I think it's best for her to hear it from me before Rick has a chance to call her and tell her half-truths or some other nonsense."

"All right. I'll let you go to do that. Call me or text me

your travel schedule so I can include it in my filing with the court."

"Will do, Bob. Thank you." Liz resolved to make sure Bob knew exactly how much she appreciated his dedication to her case. He was a one-in-a-million attorney, and she was lucky to have found him.

As she walked back to the barn to let Tiffany know she would be going back to the manor to make a private phone call, her thoughts drifted back to a happier time, when she was pregnant with Amy, and she and Rick were like most expectant parents, excited and, yes, a little anxious, about having their first child. Liz remembered how protective Rick was of her, and of the baby she carried, monitoring her health, and reading everything he could get his hands on about childbirth and baby care.

To her chagrin, Rick also was insistent that Liz give up her riding until after the baby was born. Of course, Liz knew she had to be more careful in her riding, but everything she had read and heard from other professional riders in her situation indicated that in at least the first three or four months of her pregnancy, it would be safe for the baby if she rode a normal schedule and didn't overdo it. Rick begrudgingly agreed, and the matter had been closed as far as Liz was concerned. At five months pregnant, Liz had stopped riding. There had been no visible effects on her pregnancy.

Then, at the age of three, Amy was diagnosed with cerebral palsy. Rick was certain that the cause was Liz's riding during the first four months of her pregnancy. Despite their pediatrician, obstetrician, and other specialist's assurances that his conclusions were wrong, Rick persisted in his belief that Liz's riding was the cause of Amy's disability. Ever since the diagnosis, and as Amy's symptoms became more pronounced, Rick had become more and more hostile to Liz, until it became difficult to live with him.

When Liz decided to dedicate a portion of their dressage horse training farm into a therapeutic riding practice to help Amy cope with the effects of the CP, Rick was not at all supportive. He also didn't support Liz going back into competition, so her riding career was essentially over. Despite Liz's best efforts, her marriage still suffered.

Earlier this year, saying he needed time to think, Rick moved out. It wasn't long thereafter that she was served with divorce papers. She had always felt that he would somehow come around and realize that his assumptions had been wrong, but obviously that was not going to happen.

As Liz approached the barn, she heard raised voices and followed them. As the voices became louder, she could see Tiffany in front of an open stall that contained a horse that appeared to be agitated and was acting aggressively toward one of Tiffany's barn workers. Tiffany, who was a petite 5 foot 1 or 2 inches tall, with wildly curly red hair, shoulder length, pulled back into a ponytail, was using a broom to get the horse to back away from the worker, who was trapped in a corner of stall, too terrified to move. Tiffany stood her ground and waved the broom without ever actually touching the horse and succeeded in moving him away enough that the worker was able to escape. The horse had his ears pinned back, and was baring his teeth, snapping at Tiffany and at the worker. Even though he didn't actually bite or kick anyone, it was clear that he was dangerous and couldn't be trusted.

Liz could tell that Tiffany was furious with the worker. "I told you never to approach this horse's stall without a second worker to assist." Her voice was shaking, possibly with anger, possibly a late reaction to the adrenaline rush that came with facing a life-threatening situation. "This horse was abused sometime in his past, and is very defensive when anyone enters his stall. He must always be approached by two people so that one can distract him with a treat so that the other can halter him and remove him from the stall so it can be cleaned."

The worker was clearly shaken, and appeared contrite, and Tiffany slowly cooled off as she realized the horse had also calmed once the worker had left his stall. "If this ever happens again, you will have to find another job. This is serious. You could have been killed." The worker nodded solemnly and quietly thanked Tiffany for coming to his rescue.

Liz approached Tiffany. "That was close. Are you all right?" Tiffany nodded and smiled, but Liz could tell she was still tense from the experience. "Tell me about the horse."

Tiffany led Liz back away from the stall, and looked back at the gelding, now calmly munching on his hay, clearly having recovered from his traumatic experience. "This is Rocky, which is short for Rock of Ages, his registered name. He is a thoroughbred off the track, purchased by one of Michael's long-time students, who didn't know he was abused when she bought him. He actually is a great horse to ride most of the time, but when he sees something that scares him, even under saddle, he bolts and runs uncontrollably in a panic. He's also tremendously afraid and becomes aggressively defensive when anyone tries to enter his stall. Michael agreed to take him and see if he could help him get over his fear, but it takes a great deal of time and patience to break a long-standing issue like this. Now that Michael will be riding Tempest, he may not have the time. I'm not sure what he plans to do with Rocky now."

"I'm afraid I can't be much help in this case," Liz said. "I don't have a lot of experience with abused horses."

"I understand that Michael's friend Lionel works with abused horses occasionally in his work rehabilitating off-the-track race horses. Maybe he can ask Lionel to take Rocky on." Tiffany sounded hopeful. Apparently, she had grown fond of Rocky.

Liz suddenly remembered why she had been looking for Tiffany. "I came to find you to tell you I have to go back to the manor house to Skype with my daughter, Amy. Will we see you at dinner?"

"No, I don't live here on the premises. I live in town, and take my meals at home. I will see you tomorrow."

"Yes, I'll see you then," Liz replied as she re-checked her watch.

Liz headed up to her room in the manor and located her laptop computer. Noting the time and considering the time difference, Liz knew it would be noon at home in Ohio, which was the time she and her sister Cynthia had arranged in advance for their daily communications. She knew that Amy would be waiting for her call. As she waited for the line to connect, Liz took a deep breath, and tried as best she could to school her features to be relaxed and cheerful for her conversation with her daughter.

"Hi, Mom!" Amy exclaimed excitedly as her face appeared on the screen. "How are things going today?"

"Hi, sweetie. It's good to see your smiling face." Liz couldn't help but grin indulgently back to her. Twelve-year-old Amy was the picture of youthful exuberance, her long, blond hair pulled back in to a ponytail, and her cherubic features bright with the joy of life. Even with her disability, Amy had an innate joy that transcended any negativity she might experience. Liz loved her with all her heart, and wished there was some way to make what she had to tell her easier somehow.

Her thoughts must have somehow transmitted themselves to her expression, because Amy immediately sobered. "What's wrong, Mom? You look sad."

"Nothing's wrong, sweetheart, I'm just sad that I have to be so far away from you right now." Liz tried as best she could to restore a cheerful expression, but Amy was having nothing of it.

"Dad says you're so busy, you won't have time for me, but he's wrong. I told him we talk by Skype every day, and that I tell you everything I'm doing. Aunt Cindy says I'm doing very well, and gets angry with Dad for saying bad things about you. I do too. What's wrong with him, Mom? Why is he so angry all the time?"

"I don't know why he's angry, Amy. I wish I did." Liz tried as best she could to comfort her daughter. "Where is Aunt Cindy? I need to talk to both of you right now."

"I'll get her." Amy moved away from her computer, but Liz could still hear her voice in the background. "Aunt Cindy? Can you please come here? Mom wants to talk to you."

Soon, Liz's sister Cindy appeared on the screen. "Hi, Sis, Amy told me you want to talk. I also heard Amy tell you what Rick's been saying about you while you're gone. I don't like it Liz, not one bit. Nor does Amy."

Liz sighed. "I honestly don't know why Rick has decided to cause such a problem now, but my attorney has called me to tell me he's filed a motion for full custody of Amy. He's saying I'm not a fit custodial parent because I will be out of the country for two months helping Jessica compete for Tempest.

"He hasn't said a word to me or to Amy." Cindy looked over at Amy to confirm what she was saying was accurate, and Amy shook her head no, that Rick hadn't confided his plans to her either. "But it makes sense given what he has been saying. What are you going to do, Liz?"

"I'm coming home right away," Liz responded. "Jessica's would-be sponsor is very wealthy, and owns a private jet. His sister is with us on this trip, and has committed to helping me commute back and forth from home to the UK as needed to make sure Rick can't take Amy away from me."

"How will you still be able to train Jessica if you're over here half of the time?" Cindy asked.

"With today's technology and the right equipment, I can teach Jessica by video and live feed as long as Mr. Stafford has wireless Internet capability on his farm. The only drawback is that we need Stafford's cooperation to get this done, and he's got no reason to make this easier for us. If we can't train, he wins the competition by default." Liz sighed "It looks like Rick has not only ruined my opportunity to train Jessica and help her achieve her dream, he's also made it necessary for Jessica to lose her chance as well. I'll not lose you, Amy, no matter what."

"Maybe if I talk to Dad, I can convince him not to go through with this," Amy offered.

"No, baby, I don't want you getting in the middle of this, or making your father angry. He'll probably accuse me of putting you up to it, and get ever angrier. It's better that I resolve this with him on my own."

"OK, Mom, if you say so," Amy replied, her disagreement showing in her voice. "When will you be home?"

"I expect to be home in the next day or two. Cindy, I'll send you the details when I get them. Is that all right?"

"That's fine, Liz," Cindy replied. "We'll see you soon."

"Bye, Mom. I love you. Everything will be okay." Amy smiled again at the screen.

Liz felt the tears building in her eyes, and struggled to return her daughter's cheerful smile. "I love you too, sweetie, I'll see you soon. Good-bye." She signed off and carefully put her computer away. She took a deep breath as she wiped a tear from her cheek. Rick was not going to take custody of her little girl from her. Not while she still had breath in her body. She slowly reached under her bed for her suitcase and started packing.

Chapter 10

"Excuse me, Mr. Stafford." Jessica had seen Ian Stafford walking back to the stable after turning one of Michael's horses out in a nearby pasture. She had searched the stable in vain for Michael, and didn't see him anywhere. As a last resort, she had walked outside to see if he was bringing a horse in from the pasture when she saw Ian slowly walking back to the barn.

"Call me Ian, please, Miss Warren," Ian responded. "What can I help you with?"

"I'm looking for Michael. Have you seen him? And please, if I am to call you Ian, you must call me Jessica," She responded with a hesitant smile. "I hope we can be comfortable around each other, especially since we'll be living in such close quarters for several weeks."

"All right, Jessica." Ian returned Jessica's smile. "I haven't seen Michael recently. He may have gone into town on an errand. I see his car is gone. I'm sure he'll return soon. Is there anything I can help you with?"

Jessica tried not to appear too surprised by Ian's loquaciousness. He had literally spoken less than five words to her in the week she and Liz had been living in Michael's home. "I don't think so. Now that Liz and I have arrived, and Tempest has arrived and settled in, I'd like to establish a training schedule with Michael so that we can start working with Tempest."

As if on cue, upon hearing his name mentioned, the stallion raised his head above his stall door and nickered to Jessica from down the aisle. His bright eyes revealed an intelligence that might have intimidated a less experienced rider, but Jessica was looking forward to her sessions with Tempest. With Liz helping her, Jessica had no doubt she could ride Tempest effectively.

In response to Tempest's greeting, Jessica and Ian walked down the aisle to stand in front of Tempest's stall. Jessica reached over to the stallion, allowed him to sniff her hand, then she reached over the stall door to stroke the stallion's powerfully arched neck. The stallion nickered his approval, and practically preened in pleasure at the attention. Jessica laughed.

Ian couldn't help but envy the stallion the attention Jessica was giving him. She was, after all, a very attractive woman, but in his position, a relationship with anyone would be ill advised. Still, he felt compelled to join Jessica and engage with Tempest. "So, you're a ladies' man, are you? And spoiled too, I imagine." His words were stern, but Ian was smiling. It was the first time in days that Jessica had seen Ian smile. The smile transformed his usually stern countenance to devastating effect, and Jessica could see why all Michael's female employees were half in love with Ian. He was incredibly handsome, as was Michael. But in contrast with Michael's dark good looks, Ian was blond, slightly shorter than Michael, and built like she would expect a military man to be—all muscle, and hard, steely strength. On their first day at Michael's training yard, Michael had set Jessica and Liz down and told them Ian's story. Later that day when they were introduced to Ian and had an opportunity to see him in person, the women found themselves easily believing he was innocent of the charges against him. Although reserved and solitary, Ian did not impress either of the women as being a danger to them, and they immediately accepted him as an integral part of the household.

"Do you have any idea where Michael went?" Jessica asked.

"He may have gone into town to meet with my solicitor. My movements are limited because of the ankle bracelet, but Michael can move more freely. He's trying to monitor the progress of the investigation into what happened the night of the bar fight. We're hoping he can find the woman who witnessed the whole thing, and convince her to talk to the police."

"I hope they find her soon, Ian." Jessica knew the uncertainty was taking a toll on Ian. A light sleeper, Jessica frequently heard Ian walking around the house late at night, unable to sleep. Other nights, he suffered from terrible nightmares. The first few nights after they arrived, she and Liz heard him calling out in his sleep. Usually he would call out to his friend Neil to stay down, or to stay with him hoping he wouldn't die after being shot. The experience was frightening even when Michael explained what was happening. Ian was always apologetic the next morning, and they knew he couldn't help what was happening to him, but the idea of Ian suffering without relief took an emotional toll on all of them.

"At least the National Health Service provides me with counseling. It does seem to help a bit. I'm actually doing a lot better than I was when I first arrived home from Afghanistan. Those first few months were a constant nightmare. I'm ashamed to say that I ended up relying on alcohol to numb the pain and relieve the nightmares. Unfortunately, the alcohol caused more problems than it solved. My parents couldn't live with me, and in frustration foisted me off on Michael. I'm lucky he was willing to take me in. Now this."

Neither Ian nor Jessica noticed that Michael had arrived and was walking down the aisle toward them. Michael clearly heard Ian's description of his life immediately after his return from Afghanistan, and gave Ian credit for keeping the worst of his experiences to himself. Jessica didn't have to hear every detail of Ian's struggle with PTSD, which was still a long way from resolution. Michael also found himself not liking how close Ian was standing to Jessica, enjoying her company and making her laugh. He wondered why he was feeling that way. What did it matter to him if Ian and Jessica were attracted to each other? Then it came to him. Obviously, it was because Ian was in no shape to involve himself in a relationship. His life was too chaotic, with too many loose ends. It wouldn't be wise for any woman to get involved with him right now. Yes, that had to be it.

"Actually, you showed up at just the right time, little brother." Startled by the interruption, Jessica and Ian spun around to find Michael approaching from the parking lot. "I needed more barn help, and your arrival meant I didn't have to hire someone. You're a hard worker, you're great with the horses, and I love the free help." Tempest saw Michael's arrival as an opportunity to get more attention, and nickered at him, nodding expectantly. "I see the two of you are entertaining our honored guest." He reached over and rubbed Tempest's forehead and the stallion leaned into the contact, relishing the new attention.

Jessica noticed with a tinge of envy how easily Michael and Tempest bonded. It was as if the two handsome, virile males felt an affinity with each other that she could never approach. "Michael, I'm glad you're here," Jessica said, unable to keep a note of annoyance out of her voice. "I'd like to set up a training schedule with you so that we can start working with Tempest as soon as possible."

"Certainly, Jessica. I'm happy to do that," Michael replied. He had noted Jessica's rather stiff and reserved demeanor towards him and wondered what he had done to trigger her annoyance. "I'm anxious to get started as well."

Tempest, as if sensing the conversation was about him, pawed the ground at his stall door, exhibiting his impatience to be doing something other than standing in his stall.

"I thought we could alternate days, with me riding Tempest Mondays, Wednesdays, and Fridays, and you riding him Tuesdays, Thursdays, and Saturdays. We could all have Sunday as a rest day. Since tomorrow is Monday, I'd like to begin our schedule then. Does that meet with your approval?"

"That sounds fine with me," Jessica replied. "I'll go tell Liz. I believe she's in the house calling home. Do you mind if I watch you ride?"

Michael thought a minute before answering. He was flattered that Jessica was interested in watching his rides with Tempest, but she was also the competition, and she might gain insights from watching him ride that she wouldn't gain on her own if he barred her from his training sessions. Ultimately, though, his ego won out. He actually was looking forward to having Jessica see how well he could ride Tempest. She might even ask him to help her. "Sure," he said. "I don't mind at all if you want to watch. I think Tempest likes an audience. He seemed to up his performance level when I was riding him at Mendelssohn's farm in Germany as soon as he noticed that you, Liz and Ms. McMillan had arrived."

Jessica smiled at the recollection, her annoyance disappearing. "I noticed that, too. A typical male response, if you ask me. Showing off for the ladies." Jessica teased Michael.

"I refuse to dignify that comment with an answer," Michael shot back with a smile. "I'll see you tomorrow morning, bright and early."

"It's a date," Jessica responded, then paused. She really didn't mean "date" date. It was just a figure of speech, right? She looked over at Michael to see how he had taken her response, but he was already walking back out of the barn.

Ian, however, looked at Jessica and winked. He had noticed the way Michael and Jessica had been looking at each other when they thought the other wasn't watching.

There was definitely an attraction there. Good for Michael, he thought to himself. He deserves some happiness in his life. He bid Jessica goodbye and followed Michael out of the stable.

"Hey, Mike. Wait up." Ian jogged a few strides to catch up with Michael. "What did Rogers have to say?"

Michael sighed. "He didn't have much to report. His investigator is still looking for the woman, but he hasn't gotten any solid leads yet. He's hopeful, though. The description you gave him is detailed enough that the investigator can get a sketch artist to make a likeness he can show to locals. He senses some of them are afraid of the thugs that framed you, and that's what's slowing his investigation. He's hoping to find someone who's courageous enough to give him the information he wants. He has a hunch the woman was either a current girlfriend or ex-girlfriend of one of the men that tried to assault her at the pub. They were trying to intimidate her for some reason when you got in the way."

"Bastards," Ian spat. "I could tell she knew them, and that she was scared to death of them. There's no telling what they would have done to her if I hadn't intervened. Even knowing what I do now, I would still have done it. No one deserves to be treated like that. I might have even saved her life."

"It's understandable that she's afraid to show herself. She's probably somewhere in hiding. She may not even know that you've been arrested and are being tried for manslaughter. Our only hope is that she has relatives in the town that, once they find out, can get word to her so she can help you. She must feel gratitude for what you did for her."

"When I last saw her, she was terrified, not grateful. Those men must have a powerful hold on her to make her that afraid. I'm not counting on feelings of gratitude alone to make her forget whatever it is that she's scared of."

"Rest assured, we're doing everything we can to find

her. Don't give up hope, man. This will work out." Michael tried to sound reassuring, but he knew the odds were against them. He suspected Ian realized that, too, but Michael refused to allow Ian to see him have any doubt this would all work out. It had to.

~ ~ ~

Jessica went into the manor house to find Liz and tell her what the training schedule for Tempest would be. She ran into her coming down from their rooms. "Liz, hi. Michael and I have talked, and we've worked out a training schedule for Tempest."

Liz looked distressed, and had trouble meeting Jessica's eyes. "That's great, Jess, but there's something I have to tell you."

"What's wrong, Liz? You look upset."

"I just got off the phone with my attorney, then called Amy and Cindy," Liz said. "Rick has filed in court for full custody of Amy saying that I'm not a fit mother because I've left her with Cindy for two months while we're training Tempest."

"No, Liz!" Jess exclaimed. "He can't win, can he?"

"My lawyer thinks he has a chance, unless I can get home as soon as possible, and stay home indefinitely. I'm so sorry, Jess. There is hope, though. If you're game, I might be able to train you remotely, using video and direct wireless feed. The only problem will be that Michael will have to help us, and I'm not sure he will be motivated to do that."

Michael had just entered the house and caught the last part of Jessica and Liz's conversation. The two women looked as though the world as they knew it had just ended. "Why the long faces, you two? What's happened?"

Jessica sighed. "Liz has to go back to the States to defend a custody suit by her ex-husband. She won't be able to train me and Tempest after all. Our only hope is training via video recording and possibly live stream, but we'll need your help to do it." Jessica couldn't keep the look of deep disappointment from showing on her face.

"Hmm. " Michael responded. This was certainly an interesting and positive development for his prospects with Tempest, so why wasn't he happy? Isn't this exactly what he wanted? Still, the idea of Jessica leaving the UK for good and returning to her life so far away in America didn't please him at all. Not to mention that he was actually looking forward to their mini competition. Jessica was an excellent rider, and Liz a highly respected trainer. He might actually learn something during the next two months if the competition had gone on. "Have you contacted the USDF with this new information? Maybe they can send another trainer, or find a way for Liz to teach you remotely using digital video. You have heard of YouTube, right?"

Liz started to smile. While she had discussed this possibility with her sister earlier that day, she hadn't been confident Michael would cooperate, and they needed his cooperation to pull a remote lesson schedule off. "Sure. I can do that." She looked at Michael with a combination of curiosity and pleasure. "Michael, why are you doing this? We've practically handed you Tempest, and yet you're helping us extend the competition."

Michael smiled. "Let's just say that I was looking forward to the competition. Plus, let's face it, Mendelssohn didn't seem all too keen on sponsoring me. He would prefer to sell. If you drop out of the competition, there's a good chance that he might approach the USDF and have them send another rider/trainer combination that's waiting in the wings to compete against me, and that would just delay the competition until they can get over here. I was under the impression that the sponsor buying the horse wasn't buying it specifically for you, but for the US Equestrian Team.

"You're absolutely right, Michael," Liz said. "The

USDF may very well simply send another rider and trainer to compete. Let's put our heads together and see if we can find a way to do this without giving up, Jess." Liz paused. "We've got all night. Let's get to it."

By the time the antique grandfather clock in Michael's drawing room chimed midnight, the three had worked out a seemingly doable schedule wherein Michael, with agreement from Jessica, would assist Liz in monitoring Jessica's progress directly, via phone and instant phone-linked video, and if more detailed instruction was required, via video recorded digitally and either emailed or posted to a private YouTube account only accessible to Liz, Jessica, and Michael. "I think this will work. Now, I'm going upstairs to bed. I need to get an early start to catch a plane tomorrow morning," Liz smiled weakly at both Jessica and Michael and headed up the stairs. "Jess, are you coming?"

"I'll be right up, Liz," Jessica responded. "You go ahead. There's something I want to talk to Michael about."

"All right," Liz replied, looking a bit puzzled, "Good night. Both of you." She pointedly looked a Michael as if to warn him from taking advantage of Jessica in her semi-exhausted state, then disappeared above stairs.

Michael himself was puzzled as to the reason Jessica needed to speak with him alone. "What is it, Jessica?"

Jessica's brilliant green eyes looked directly into Michael's, with a serious, determined stare. "Why are you doing this, Michael? You had the opportunity to win this competition without any more effort than to spend some time riding Tempest until the two of you worked as one. Why are you giving me this chance?"

Michael returned Jessica's gaze, immediately mesmerized by her beautiful eyes and the sincerity in them. They showed she wasn't trying to hide her feelings or deceive him in any way. She just wanted a simple answer to a simple question. The problem was, could he give her one? Did he know the true reason why he had offered to help her, and why he couldn't seem to let her go back home just yet? He fumbled a bit, but fell back on the excuse that he had given her and Liz earlier. "It was clear to me that Mendelssohn wasn't interested in sponsoring me as long as there was a possibility that Tempest could be sold. The fact that the USDF has found a sponsor willing to spend the money to buy a horse for the USET means that if you were not able to take advantage of the opportunity, there would very well be someone else standing in the wings that could. Now that I've met you and Liz, I like you, and don't want to go through this 'competition' with anyone else. Not to mention that if we had to start over again, the entire matter would be delayed, which wouldn't help anyone in the long run. It just made sense."

Jessica searched Michael's face for any sign that he was prevaricating, but his willingness to meet her gaze without wavering showed he was sincere. He really wanted to do this, for her and Liz, yes, but also because he understood the competition they represented and felt comfortable with it. That part of his answer didn't make her feel much better, but in some ways his answer comforted her. She could tell from this brief interaction that Michael wouldn't withhold the truth from her if she were to ask for it, and that was important for their relationship going forward.

"Thank you, Michael. Both Liz and I are grateful that you're willing to help." To Michael's surprise, Jessica stood up on her tiptoes and kissed him briefly on the cheek, then she smiled shyly, spun around, and darted up the stairs.

Michael touched the place where she had kissed him with the tips of his fingers and felt a bit of moisture and the vague imprint of Jessica's lips as the memory of the kiss warmed him. He smiled to himself. This was going to be an interesting two months. At the same time, he found himself wondering why that prospect didn't bother him in the least.

Chapter 11

Michael's first training day dawned clear and sunny. Temperatures were a bit above normal, so Michael chose to ride in the outdoor arena rather than the indoor. He knew he risked Tempest being a bit more energetic working outside, but his experience riding Romeo had prepared him for almost anything a mischievous stallion could throw at him. Riding helmet firmly in place, he led Tempest out to the arena and approached the mounting block. Suddenly, Tempest lifted his handsome head and nickered to someone approaching the arena. Michael followed the horse's gaze and saw Jessica approaching from the house. She was wearing jeans that fit her long, slim legs to perfection, and a crisp, white polo shirt open at the collar. Her long, mahogany-brown hair, was pulled back into a simple ponytail. As she approached, he noticed the sun magnified the red and gold highlights. Michael couldn't help wondering if her hair was as soft and thick as it looked. He caught himself imagining his fingers running through it, and quickly pulled his thoughts back, hoping that the flash of desire he felt didn't show in his expression. He schooled his features to present what he hoped was a neutral but friendly look.

"Good morning," Jessica called. "I hope you don't mind having an audience."

"I didn't expect you to be up so early," Michael said. "I hope you've had breakfast."

"I did. You have a very well-stocked kitchen, so I made myself some eggs and toast. I also tried to make coffee with your French press. I'll need to work on that. I made it way too strong." She blushed, rather becomingly, he thought.

"I'm sorry to hear that," Michael responded. "I'll give you a lesson once I'm done here. In answer to your question, certainly you can watch. Have a seat on the bleachers and enjoy."

"Thanks!" She climbed about halfway up the small set of bleachers next to the outdoor arena and made herself comfortable, or as comfortable as you can get on a backless, aluminum seat.

While the two had been talking, Tempest began to lose patience, and exhibited his frustration by fidgeting in place, clearly bored and eager to start working. Of course, he also wanted to demand more attention for himself.

"Easy, boy, I'm coming." Michael reluctantly turned his attention away from Jessica, tried to soothe the stallion's slightly bruised ego, quickly mounted him, adjusted his seat, checked the length of his stirrup leathers and began to get an overall feel for the horse. It had been almost 2 weeks since he had last ridden Tempest, and he wanted to take a few minutes to get reacquainted with him. It appeared Tempest wasn't quite done showing Michael his displeasure at being made to wait to start work. The stallion tensed his back and crow-hopped a few times, testing Michael's resolve and his abilities right from the start. Michael responded by immediately putting Tempest into a canter, and accelerated to a hand gallop, covering the perimeter of the arena in large, ground-eating strides, until Tempest finally relaxed and Michael could then bring him back to a smooth, rolling canter. "That was a test," Michael called out to Jessica, who had been watching the stallion's behavior with some concern.

"You handled him beautifully," Jessica called back. "I agree that he needed a good gallop to get the kinks out." She didn't let on how afraid she had been for Michael's safety. Nor would she let on that after seeing Tempest demonstrate his prowess at being naughty in an attempt to test a new rider, she was more than a little apprehensive about how she would react when, not if, that powerful horse would test her.

The rest of the ride was relatively uneventful. Michael put Tempest through some more basic collected work and made sure the stallion knew he could handle the occasional hint at rebellion. Overall, he considered the day a success. Tomorrow he would observe and possibly assist Jessica in her first ride. He was very much looking forward to it.

~ ~ ~

The following day also dawned sunny and from all appearances would be just as warm as the previous day. Jessica woke up early, dressed in her breeches and polo shirt, pulled on her socks then boots, and made her way to the main floor for breakfast. She was surprised to see Michael already in the breakfast room waiting for her.

"Good morning," he greeted her warmly. "I hope you slept well."

"I did," Jessica lied. She had been tossing and turning most of the night, worried about how Tempest would react to her since he had unseated her the last time she rode him. "I have to admit that I'm more than a little nervous about my first ride on Tempest since Germany, though."

"My advice would be to approach him as if this was your first encounter, and make sure you project confidence. Establish the boundaries with him from the very beginning. Remember, stallions are always looking for ways to challenge your authority. You can't let him have an inch, or he will take it and try for more."

"Right." Jessica couldn't keep a slight note of trepidation from coming through her voice.

"If you like, I can get on him first, and warm him up a bit for you."

Even though a part of her welcomed the offer, Jessica felt she was being condescended to, and bristled at the implication in Michael's offer that she couldn't handle Tempest on her own. She lifted her chin in a sign of defiance and said, "No thanks, I can do this."

Michael noted the tension emanating from Jessica, and realized his offer had likely crossed a line. He never would have offered to warm up a horse for a male professional rider, and she probably knew that. She took offense because it seemed on the surface he was treating her like a weak, inexperienced female, and he couldn't blame her for being offended. Truly, he meant no offense. He was only trying to help. She even told him she was nervous about her first ride. If Jessica had known him for longer than a week, she would have known that his offer was meant to be helpful, not as an insult. As it was, she took his offer the wrong way. Probably best to retreat for now, and look for an opportunity later today to try to make things right. "Fine. Get something to eat, and meet me in the stable. I have to check in with Tiffany and see how the other horses are doing." He left the breakfast area and walked out the front door toward the stables.

"Fine," Jessica said. She found the eggs and toast and decided to try the French press again to perfect her coffee making skills. Inwardly, she berated herself for overreacting and losing her temper with Michael. *What were you thinking, Jess?* There's no way Michael was going to follow up on his offer to help her after she had just bitten his head off. How could she have talked to him like that? Deep down she knew his offer didn't come from condescension and that he was only trying to help. In truth, it was probably a good idea for Michael to warm Tempest up for her the first time she rode him in two weeks. She should have agreed. True, it was hard not being self-conscious and nervous in the presence of a bona fide Olympic champion. Now, she'd just pretty much told him she was too good to ask for his help. For goodness' sake! Where did that come from?

Out in the stable, Michael checked in with Tiffany, looked in on his other horses, and went to Tempest's stall to start getting him ready.

"Wait," Jessica called as she approached from down the aisle, "I'd like to groom him and tack him up to get him used to me. Is that all right?"

"Sure. It's a good idea, actually. While you're doing that, I'll set up the video recording equipment so we can record your ride for Liz."

"Great!" Jessica's smile was the most relaxed and genuine one he'd seen from her, and it dazzled him. *I guess she must have forgiven me for my blunder.* If he thought she was beautiful before, her heartfelt smile transformed her into the most beautiful woman he had ever seen. And he had seen many.

When Michael turned away to find the video equipment, Jessica sighed with relief. It seemed Michael hadn't held her little demonstration of pique against her, and was willing to give her the benefit of the doubt. She visibly relaxed and prepared to take Tempest out of his stall and tack him up. "Hey, big boy," Jessica greeted the big, black stallion. "Are you ready to go to work?" Tempest nickered at her, and seemed to nod his big head in agreement. Jessica laughed. "I'll hold you to that." Jessica grew serious as she looked into Tempest's eyes while putting on the halter. "Be nice to me, big guy, all right? I really want to show Michael that I know what I'm doing, and that I deserve to be here. Can you cooperate for me today?" Tempest pawed the ground in a sign of impatience to get started, and Jessica led him to the cross ties.

After Tempest was saddled, Jessica walked him to the mounting block, mounted and entered the outdoor arena. Tempest immediately tensed underneath her as he noticed something new at the end of the arena. Michael had set up the video camera on a tripod in the center of one of the short sides of the arena to capture the entire arena on screen. Michael, unbeknownst to Jessica, had arranged for one of his barn workers to man the video camera, so the camera could zoom in when Jessica was at the far end of the arena away from the camera. Michael positioned himself in the center of the arena so he could assist Jessica if she needed it.

"If you don't want me here, I'll leave," Michael offered. Jessica could tell that he was still a little wary of asserting himself too much after their interchange earlier that morning.

"No. Actually, I like that you're here, at least for my first time in the saddle," Jessica responded, purposely offering a bit of an olive branch to Michael. She nudged Tempest forward toward the scary video set up, and allowed him to take a good look at it before asking him to move on. The stallion snorted at the camera once, then his curiosity got the better of him, and he stretched his nose out to try to sniff the camera. The worker behind the camera smiled and spoke to Tempest to let him know there was a person there, too. After satisfying himself that the camera wasn't a monster ready to devour him, Tempest settled down, and Jessica could feel his body relax underneath her. She tried to remember what Liz had told her that day in Germany when she first rode Tempest, and started out with a relaxed, forward trot to warm both of them up.

"His favorite gait appears to be his canter," Michael called. "It might be better to warm him up there, first."

"I'd prefer to work him in the trot first," Jessica called back. "I really want to get him stretching through his back at the trot before I try a canter."

"Fine," Michael called back, smiling to himself. She was a woman with a mind of her own. He liked that. To be honest, the canter was Michael's favorite gait to ride, so he might have started his warm-up in the canter just because it made him more comfortable, and Tempest just didn't object. Her reasoning for not going along with his suggestion was good, too. He must remember that even though she was younger than he, she had a lot of experience, and was an excellent rider. This wasn't one of his adult amateur students.

As they worked, Jessica felt a little uncomfortable in the saddle. Something appeared to be wrong with her stirrup length. She called out to Michael. "Can you see if my stirrup leathers are the same length? They feel uneven. My right stirrup feels longer than my left."

She stopped, and Michael stood directly in front of Tempest and compared the two stirrup lengths. "You're right. The right stirrup is one hole longer than the left. Let me fix it."

"You don't have to do that. I can fix it." Jessica shifted her right leg back, and started to reach down to move the stirrup leathers. Michael was already there, and fixed the leather himself. When he shortened the leather a notch, he took Jessica's right thigh in both hands and moved it back into place on the saddle. A bolt of awareness shot through Jessica at his touch, and she trembled a bit at her strong reaction. Michael's eyes flashed desire before he masked his expression to appear nonchalant about touching her, and Jessica thought he held her leg for just a bit longer than he had to. He slid his hands down her thigh a few inches before letting go, a movement that wasn't really necessary. She didn't say anything, though. It actually felt very pleasurable.

"Thanks." Jessica's eyes met Michael's and she thought she saw a hint of a more than friendly interest before he broke away and stepped back.

"My pleasure." The corners of Michael's lips turned up in a very slight smile, and his eyes sparked with mischief before he walked away.

Now that her stirrups were balanced, she completed their warmup then put Tempest through a few collected movements and spent some time getting a feel for how he behaved under saddle. Today, there were no scary moments, and Jessica's confidence grew as she was able to successfully execute large parts of an Intermediare I test. When she finished, Michael complemented her on her handling of the stallion.

"You did really well, Jess. Liz will be happy to see your performance today."

"How soon will she be able to see the video?" Jessica asked.

"I should be able to upload it today," Michael replied. "You may even be able to discuss your ride with Liz before dinner."

While Michael was busy uploading her video onto YouTube, Jessica placed a call to her sister, Hailey.

"Jess!" Hailey exclaimed upon answering her cell phone. "I'm so glad you called. How are things going over there?"

"Things are great, squirt, but I have some news. Liz is heading home." Jessica checked her watch and did a quick calculation. "Actually, she should be there by now. Her flight left Heathrow about eight hours ago."

"What happened, Jess? Is the competition over already?" Hailey's concern was evident.

Jessica rushed to correct Hailey's misperception. "No, not at all. It's just that Rick has just filed a motion with the divorce court for full custody of Amy, and is trying to use the fact that Liz is spending sixty days here in the UK with me to try to prove to the court that she's an unfit mother."

"What a jerk!" Hailey responded. "So how are you going to train with Tempest when Liz is over here?"

"Michael was kind enough to set up a video camera to record our sessions, and upload them to YouTube so Liz can watch them and give me training advice. It's not ideal, but it's better than nothing."

"*Michael*, eh?" Hailey said. "You're getting pretty cozy with Mr. Stafford, aren't you, Sis? I really can't blame you for falling for him, though. There's no denying he's gorgeous."

Jessica felt herself blush. This was the second time she had been teased about her familiarity with Michael. "That's not how things are, Hailey. Michael is just being kind. He already had the video equipment here, and it's not that big a deal to set it up." Jessica didn't mention that Michael had also arranged for one of his barn staff to man the video recorder and that he was personally uploading the video to the Internet for her. Hailey didn't need to know all of that, did she?

"I wish I could be there with you, Jess," Hailey said. "This is my last week of school, and it's going to be really lonely around here with you gone."

"You know, now that Liz isn't staying here, it's kind of lonely for me, too," Jessica replied. "Maybe I'll check with Charlotte McMillan and see if her brother is willing to fly you over here on his private jet. If he has business in the UK anyway, it wouldn't be an extra trip to bring you as well."

"Really, Jess? You'd do that for me?" Hailey's excitement was infectious. "That would be great!"

"I'll call Charlotte tomorrow and ask. The worst that can happen is she says no. But first, I'll call your therapist and make arrangements for you to continue your therapy here in the UK. Until I get that arranged, just keep doing what you've been doing. You need to stay in shape if you ever want to try to play soccer again with prosthetic legs."

"Thanks, Jess. You're the greatest."

Just at that moment, Michael appeared at Jessica's bedroom door and signaled that the video had been uploaded. Jessica smiled and mouthed the words "thank you" then returned to her phone call.

"I've got to go now, Hailey. I'll call you tomorrow after I've talked to Charlotte. Hopefully, I'll have an answer tomorrow."

"Bye, Jess, and thank you! I'm so excited!" Jessica heard a squeal on the other end of the line before Hailey hung up.

Jessica ended the call and looked over at Michael. "I hope you don't mind, but I just invited my sister Hailey to come over here and stay with us, if she can get a ride on Blake McMillan's private jet in the next week or two."

Michael wondered if Jessica realized that her characterization of herself and Michael as "us" made it sound as though they were a couple. At the same time, he was amazed that the idea of himself and Jessica as a couple, living here together in his home, didn't bother him in the least. Most likely because that eventuality would never happen, he concluded. He was painfully aware of how his recently earned reputation as a hard partier and womanizer had tainted his image in the dressage world. Best not to dwell on what could never happen.

Chapter 12

The following week, Jessica watched from her bedroom window as Michael took his turn working with Tempest. Herr Mendelssohn was there also, watching intently as the two worked. Jessica couldn't take her eyes off the pair as they worked through a Grand Prix Special test. Just as they had in Germany, Michael and Tempest looked as if they had been working together for years, not days.

Jessica also couldn't help but be drawn to the raw masculinity of Michael as he sat tall and proud aboard the magnificent stallion and made the intricate movements of Grand Prix dressage appear effortless, when Jessica knew they were not. She knew from her experience riding Tempest that he could be strong and he was intelligent enough to come up with creative evasions that made riding him a constant mental and physical challenge. Jessica also noticed that Herr Mendelssohn seemed very impressed with the work Michael was doing with Tempest. That meant that her challenge in proving herself more worthy of Tempest than Michael was clearly going to be even more difficult than she originally thought.

At least Hailey was coming, and would keep her company through this. Jessica had spoken with Charlotte, who easily agreed to send Hailey over two weeks from today. Jessica was grateful to Charlotte and her brother Blake for their kindness to her and Hailey. They made it seem so easy to make what otherwise would have been very complicated arrangements. Jessica was just beginning to realize how much she missed Hailey in just the past week away from home. Jessica had been honest with Hailey when she told her she was lonely. Without Liz here with her, Jessica didn't have anyone to talk to, no one to confide her fears and insecurities to. She certainly wasn't going to reveal them to Michael or Herr Mendelssohn and especially not to Michael's friend Lionel. This was a competition after all, and none of them had her best interests at heart.

~ ~ ~

Today it was Jessica's turn to train with Tempest, and Michael was there, eager to watch. The weather wasn't cooperating very well, with rain in the forecast, so Jessica's work session moved into the indoor arena. The video camera was set up inside, and Tempest again appeared nervous about the strange appearance. This time, Jessica was having a hard time getting Tempest to relax, and Michael suggested she allow the stallion to gallop around the arena to let out the excess energy in a more productive way. Jessica hesitated at first, thinking the last things she wanted was to be aboard a 1500-pound animal hurtling itself around the arena in a barely controllable state, but she was beginning to trust Michael's judgment and sent Tempest forward. She could feel the stallion collect himself underneath her then rocket forward. Jessica leaned forward to make as low a profile as possible and still maintain some control. It didn't take long for Jessica to feel comfortable with Tempest's ground-eating gallop, and she had time to contemplate the amount of power the stallion had. Even at a gallop, the horse demonstrated self-carriage and suspension, and he felt lighter than air to ride. After three good circuits around the arena, Jessica found to her surprise that Tempest had calmed significantly, and that she did have a great deal of control over the stallion. She slowed her seat and gradually brought Tempest back to an easy working canter.

"What do you think?" Michael was smiling at her, because he knew exactly how that experience felt.

"All I can say is *Wow!*" Jessica replied. "What a ride!" She knew she was grinning ear to ear, and her confidence level soared. *Michael did this for me.* She thought to herself. *He knew that Tempest would relax if he were allowed to gallop, and that I was going to have the ride of my life.* Jessica's nerves had disappeared completely, and they were ready to work. Tempest's fears of the video camera were a thing of the past. He hardly noticed anything beyond Jessica on his back. They had a spectacular work session, focusing on passage and piaffe, as well as the other more collected movements since Tempest had energy to burn this day.

When they were finished, and after Jessica had untacked Tempest and put him away in his stall, she approached Michael, who had been waiting for her at the entryway to the barn. "Thank you for what you did out there, Michael. Even though you have only known Tempest and me for two weeks, you knew exactly what we both needed to get past his spookiness. You're a great trainer. I'm surprised you don't have more students coming here to learn from you."

Michael hesitated then cleared his throat "I decided to focus my efforts on developing another international class horse for myself, and dedicated my time to those pursuits instead." Even to him that sounded false, and he hoped Jessica was gullible enough to believe his rather flimsy lie.

"I see," Jessica said skeptically. She had heard of the rumors about Michael, but realized after his response that he wasn't willing to talk about what the rumor mill had labeled his "dark period." "What happened with that? You obviously weren't successful, or you wouldn't be competing for Tempest."

"No. I wasn't successful, at least not in finding my next competition horse," Michael responded. "But I have developed two horses I can market and sell to talented adult amateur riders. Come down here and let me introduce you to my 'projects.'"

Michael led Jessica down the aisle and they made a ninety-degree right turn to enter the aisle that housed Michael's horses, and the horses of a small number of boarders. He stopped in front of a stall that housed a 17-hand chestnut gelding with a white blaze and a curious and intelligent look in his eyes. "This is Monty. He's a seven-year-old Danish Warmblood with spectacular bloodlines. Unfortunately, he doesn't have the fire necessary to compete at the Grand Prix level internationally. He has a spectacular canter and a respectable trot, but his walk is problematic. He will make some adult amateur a great competition horse, though. He also has a fantastic personality and a great work ethic. He's just fun to ride. Unfortunately, I can't keep a horse just because he's fun. He's for sale right now."

Jessica reached over the stall door to scratch Monty on the nose. He snuffled at her hand, and snorted gently. "He's so cute!" Jessica laughed. "It's a shame he doesn't have a permanent home yet. Let me ask around and see if I know anyone who might be interested."

Just then, the horse in the next stall, seeing Monty getting attention, nickered at Michael and stuck her head out over her stall door. She was a dark bay mare with a black mane and tail and a white star on her forehead. "This is Abby," Michael said. "She is a Dutch Warmblood mare I also purchased as a prospect, but alas, she also isn't working out. Abby would rather stay at home than perform for a crowd. She gets so nervous at shows that she won't eat, and paces in her stall so much, I fear when she does eat, she might colic. She would make a wonderful brood mare, though, and I sometimes use her as a school horse because she is very patient and not easily spooked.

"She is so sweet," Jessica exclaimed, as Abby nuzzled her and rested her large head against Jessica's shoulder. "All she wants to do is snuggle." She smiled at Michael, who was immediately entranced. Any words he might have said in response were stuck in his throat.

Ian's voice came to them from down the aisle. "It looks like you've made a couple of friends today." Michael and Jessica looked up to see Ian approaching. "It's time for these two to go out for some pasture time." Ian looked at Jessica and winked. "This is my way of earning my keep while I'm staying here mooching off of my big brother."

Michael felt a stab of irritation at the way Ian was obviously flirting with Jessica, and at the implication that he was a burden on Michael. As a result, his attitude toward Ian was gruff. "Ian, you're not mooching. I'm happy to have you staying with me." Michael's demeanor softened as he turned to Jessica. "It is time for these two to go out. Let's go back to the house and see what the video from today's session looks like."

"Certainly." Jessica smiled. "I'm anxious to see how the passage and piaffe looked. They felt spectacular."

"They were," Michael replied. "It's too bad Herr Mendelssohn wasn't here to see it. He had to go back to Germany and his breeding farm. There was too much going on in anticipation of the next auction at Verden. He felt he should be there."

"Oh," Jessica said, disappointed. "I had hoped he would be able to watch our progress in person. Will you send him links to the training sessions along with Liz?"

"That's my plan. Does that work for you?"

"Yes. I suppose a video is better than nothing at all. Most certainly."

"My thoughts exactly. That means, however, that you have to supervise the taping of my riding sessions as well. Will that be all right?"

"Sure. That will be fine. I'm looking forward to it. Do you mind if I ask questions while you're riding? I might learn something from you as well."

Flattered that a rider as good as Jessica expected to learn from him, Michael said, "Certainly. I have no objection whatsoever. Ask away."

As they turned away from Ian to make their way back to the house, Michael instinctively reached his hand toward the small of Jessica's back unconsciously staking his claim on her. Realizing what he was doing, he stopped himself at the last second. He looked back at Ian to see his brother grinning at him. Damn his brother for seeing what Michael was trying to ignore. He was attracted to Jessica like he hadn't been attracted to a woman since Emma. He was going to have to resist this attraction. It reminded him too much of how he felt about Emma before she betrayed him. He was definitely in dangerous territory.

Jessica's body hummed with awareness when Michael's hand came oh so close to touching the small of her back, then retreated. She looked up at Michael, who was determinedly trying to avoid meeting her eyes. She tried desperately to think of something to talk about that would break the tension that had suddenly appeared between them when Michael's friend Lionel drove up.

"Lionel!" Michael called. "It's good to see you. What brings you by this fine day?"

"Actually, I'm here to meet the horse you asked me to look at that needs rehabilitation." *And I have been away from this situation far too long. I need to observe the situation and make plans accordingly.*

"Ah, yes. I do recall telling you about Rocky." Grateful for the interruption, Michael turned to Jessica. "Before we look at the video, I'd like to take Lionel in to see Rocky. Do you mind?"

"Of course not," Jessica replied. "I'll just call my sister and check in. Take all the time you need."

"Thanks." Michael's smile was genuine, and the tension between them had disappeared. "I'll be in as soon as I can."

Jessica nodded and made her way back to the house. Was she mistaken, or was Michael fighting his attraction to her. Jessica hadn't been in a serious romantic relationship since her longtime boyfriend broke up with her soon after her parents' accident, but she wasn't so naive or inexperienced with men that she couldn't tell that Michael was as attracted to her as she was to him. Why the resistance? Maybe he thought she wasn't good enough for him. Of course, that's it. It made sense. He's an internationally famous dressage rider acknowledged to be one of the world's most beautiful people. What could he see in a small-town Ohio girl who was only marginally pretty, and not nearly as sophisticated and worldly as the women he most likely attracted. Or, maybe he had looked into her background and learned about the details surrounding the accident that had claimed her parents' lives and injured Hailey. Jessica shook her head. No, he couldn't know that. If Michael had known everything about her, he wouldn't even be speaking to her, let alone volunteering to train her, or allowing himself to be attracted to her. As much as it hurt her to do it, Jessica resolved not to encourage Michael's affections. She was not worthy of someone like him.

Chapter 13

"So, how are things going with Tempest?" Lionel asked.

"Great, actually," Michael responded. "He's a great horse, with tremendous talent. He just needs someone to challenge him. He's so very intelligent, and therefore very easily bored, and when he gets bored, he gets naughty, making up ways to test his rider. He's tried it with both Jessica and me."

"So, is Jessica coping well with him? I didn't think she was capable enough to handle him after he misbehaved and threw her in Germany."

"Actually, Jessica is quite a capable rider. She has the talent and guts to ride Tempest. Her only weakness in my view is her lack of international competition experience. I don't think she has any idea how cutthroat some of the competition can be at these events."

Lionel noticed right away that Michael's offer to step in and help Jessica train with Tempest had brought them closer together, and might lead to a training job for Michael even if he didn't win the competition for Tempest. The more time they spent together working with Tempest, the more likely the competition might end up benefitting both of them. This concerned him. There had to be something he could do to disrupt the positive momentum. He would have to think about it. Maybe he could spend a few days and figure something out. He could not let Michael succeed in any way in this competition.

Michael and Lionel approached a stall somewhat separate from the others in Michael's wing of the barn. "Here's the horse I was telling you about. Say hello to Rocky." Michael moved to the front of a stall. Inside was a rather dull-looking bay gelding, about 16 hands tall, with a nondescript star on his forehead. Lionel noticed that there didn't appear to be any marks on the horse, but he appeared to tense and pin his ears when anyone approached the door of his stall.

"My student, Corrine, bought Rocky as a trail horse for her daughter, Samantha. When they went to test ride the horse, he had already been taken out of stall, and appeared to be fine. He was comfortable to ride and his price was very reasonable, so she bought him. The first sign of trouble came when they came back a few days later to pick him up, and it took them two hours to load him in their trailer. Finally, the seller took a large whip and chased him into the trailer. When they got him home, other signs of trouble showed up.

It became clear that the sellers had drugged Rocky so he behaved calmly while being ridden. In reality, he is fearful of being touched, and threatens to bite or kick anyone who comes into his stall unless he is distracted by either another person, with an offering of an apple, carrot or other treat. It's clear that his previous owners abused him. In addition, the horse has no confidence or trust in his rider, and is dangerous to ride. On trail rides, if a rabbit jumps out, or a plastic bag blows across the trail, he bolts away at a dead run, and can't be controlled. Corrine is ready to have him put down, but I talked her into allowing you to look at him and see if there's anything you can do."

Lionel felt rage building within him as he listened to Michael's description of the behaviors Rocky exhibited. "The bastards should be shot for treating a sensitive animal that way. I definitely want to see if there's anything I can do to help. I'll do it gladly."

"Excellent!" Michael said. "I'll contact Corrine and let her know you'll be working with Rocky for the next few weeks. She'll be thrilled, especially if you can make some progress with him."

"Don't get her hopes up too high, mate," Lionel cautioned. "Fear is a powerful emotion, and Rocky has been ruled by fear for quite some time. It will take a great deal of time and patience to convince him he doesn't have anything to be afraid of. You have a round pen I can use, don't you?"

"Yes. You're welcome to use it any time," Michael replied. "Will you be staying here, or will you be driving back and forth from your farm?"

"If possible, I'd like to stay here for the first few days, to really get to know Rocky. Do you have a place for me?"

"Actually, I do. Herr Mendelssohn left to go back to Germany, so you can use his room while you're here. Jessica is actually the only other person staying here right now. Her trainer, Liz Randall, had to go back to the States for a personal emergency. Jessica is communicating with her via YouTube and Skype right now."

"Really," Lionel said. "That's a new development. What's the 'personal emergency?'"

"I'm really not at liberty to say, Lionel," Michael said. "Suffice it to say that it's more important for Liz to be in the U.S. than here for the time being."

"All right," Lionel said. "If you don't mind, I'd like to spend a few minutes alone here with Rocky, and see just exactly what we have here. Then, maybe we can go to the pub for dinner?"

"Actually, Lionel, I was planning to take Jessica out for dinner tonight," Michael said, clearly chagrined at sharing this information with Lionel before he had a chance to ask Jessica. He reluctantly added, "I suppose you could come along, though."

Lionel smiled to himself at the grudging manner in which Michael had, only out of sheer politeness, asked Lionel to accompany him and Jessica for dinner. Feigning ignorance of Michael's discomfort, Lionel enthusiastically responded. "Of course. I'd love to join you. It will give me an opportunity to learn more about Jessica, especially since I'll be staying here at the manor for a few days. If you don't mind, though, I'd like to drive separately. I have a couple of errands to run while I'm out."

"No problem. We'll look forward to it," Michael responded, less than enthusiastically, as he made his way back to the house.

Lionel, finally on his own, made his way to the stable, and immediately looked not for Rocky, but for Tempest's stall. It wasn't hard to find. Michael had fashioned a larger than normal-sized box stall for Tempest, with more than the usual stall accouterments, including a beautiful leather halter with shiny brass hardware and his name engraved in gold plate on the cheek strap hanging on the front of the stall. A brass nameplate with his name engraved along with his breed logo graced the stall door.

The stallion himself looked up at Lionel's approach and graced him with a curious but guarded expression. Lionel approached with a measure of caution. He had worked with stallions before, and they could be unpredictable and frequently aggressive. Not to mention that he was, to this stallion, a relative stranger. He needn't have worried, however. This stallion had never in his life experienced even one incident of abuse, and was accustomed to being handled by professionals whose primary interest was keeping him content. His general trust in and comfort around people overcame any fear that a sudden appearance by a stranger at his stall might otherwise provoke.

"My boy, you are a beauty." Lionel found himself in awe at this magnificent horse. "It's too bad your interests and mine are at odds. I would love to see you shown by someone who knows what they're doing, and Michael is absolutely that person." Feeling more than a slight twinge of regret at what he had to do, Lionel looked around the stable to see if there was any way he might arrange for a small accident for Tempest that would impair both Michael and Jessica's ability to ride him for the next few weeks. In Lionel's estimation, such an accident would be all it would take to convince Herr Mendelssohn that neither Michael nor Jessica were to be trusted with his precious stallion, and Mendelssohn would take him home to Germany to look for another match.

Unfortunately, Michael kept an immaculate stable, and there was nothing lying around that would cause an injury such as Lionel might need for his purposes. Lionel noted the grain room was just down the aisle from Tempest's stall, and when he tried the door, it was unlocked. *Brilliant!* All I have to do is open the grain room door, ensure a grain bin is left open, and unlatch Tempest's stall door. In that way, once Tempest smelled the unmistakable odor of molasses, and realized the grain was available for the taking, he would be able to easily open his stall door, and make his way to the grain to feast to his heart's content. Better yet, there wouldn't be any clear evidence of wrongdoing.

The fact that Tempest's stall was left unlatched could easily be blamed on a careless barn worker. To ensure that Tempest didn't eat so much grain that the damage would be life-threatening, he would wake up within an hour of retiring, ostensibly having heard a noise, and discovered Tempest in time to save his life. His timely "discovery" would ensure that the horse got enough grain in him to only cause a mild if any, colic, or a mild case of laminitis, an inflammation of the feet caused by too much rich feed hitting his system in a short period of time. The only treatment for such an affliction was stall rest in deep footing and inactivity for as long as the inflammation persists. The plan was set. "I'll be back to see you later tonight, boy," Lionel said with a grin. "I hope you'll be hungry."

Later that evening, as Michael was driving Jessica back to the manor from the pub where he, Jessica and Lionel had partaken of a somewhat strained dinner, he realized that Jessica hadn't said a word since they left the pub. He glanced over at her as she sat next to him in the passenger seat, and noticed that she was staring out of the side window, but her gaze wasn't focused, and he could tell that she was mentally miles away. "You're very quiet this evening, Jess. Is something wrong?"

Michael's attempt at conversation had startled Jessica out of her reverie, and she looked guiltily over at Michael, flushing with embarrassment that he had caught her daydreaming. "It's nothing, really," Jessica said. "I'm just worried about Hailey. I've been trying to contact her physical therapist and doctor to get recommendations for physicians and therapists here in the UK so that she can continue her fitness and rehabilitation, but they're not returning my calls. It's very frustrating, and there's nothing I can do about it when I'm over here, four thousand miles away."

"Does it have to be done right now?" Michael asked. "After all, we can always look into those possibilities once Hailey gets here. In fact, it might be better if she meets with the potential doctors and therapists before committing to anyone to make sure they're compatible."

"We?" Jessica asked, suddenly irritated that Michael was taking it upon himself to assume part of a responsibility that had been Jessica's, and Jessica's alone, for the past 5 years. "Michael, this isn't your obligation, it's mine. And yes, it does have to be done now. I would rather have arrangements made up front, before Hailey gets here so she won't miss any therapy. It's critical for her long-term progress that she continue being active and that she maintain a constant level of care." Jessica felt the anger rising within her, and her next statement was laced with sarcasm. "Of course, not having ever had to experience something like this, you wouldn't know that." Seeing the stricken look on Michael's face after that statement, Jessica immediately regretted her angry reaction, and softened in response, "Please, Michael, I know you mean well, but this is none of your business."

Michael was taken aback by the vehemence of Jessica's reaction to his offer to help, and to what he considered to be a common-sense solution to her problem. He realized that there was more to Jessica's relationship with Hailey and her injuries than what appeared on the surface. He resolved to discover what it was that made Jessica so very protective and determined to "fix" Hailey. He wondered if there was any way for him to really help her, or if she would have to resolve those issues herself. What he did know was that she couldn't continue to allow Hailey's condition to rule her own life. At some point, probably very soon, Hailey would be old enough to be on her own, and Jessica would have to let her go. For now, though, it was time to change the subject.

"Lionel said he had some errands to run, then he would be back to the house. Are you comfortable with him staying here for a few days?"

"Michael, it's your home, and Lionel is your friend. I should have no say in whether he stays or goes, but since you're asking me, I'm fine with him being here. I do have to admit, though, that he makes me uncomfortable, but I can't for the life of me tell you why."

"He's had a hard life, but I've known him for years, and trust him. I think he's Rocky's last chance at redemption. I'm very much hoping he can find a way to bring that poor horse back and make him a decent riding horse."

"For Rocky's sake, I agree with you. No horse deserves to be abused."

Chapter 14

It was midnight when Lionel drove up to the house, and saw that every window was dark. No one stirred. This was the perfect time to implement his plan. He quietly entered the barn, and made his way to the grain room. Thankfully, the room was still unlocked, and the sweet feed easily accessed. He propped the lid of the large dustbin sized container, at least half-filled with grain, and left the room, door ajar. He made his way to Tempest's stall and unhooked the latch keeping the door closed.

Tempest watched Lionel's movements with interest, but didn't immediately move to test the stall door. "Just wait until you get a whiff of that good, sweet grain, and you'll be desperate to get there. I've just made it easier for you to have what you want, my boy. Enjoy!" Lionel smiled to himself as he left the barn, and quietly entered the manor. He moved up the stairs as silently as possible and made his way to his assigned bedroom. There, he undressed, and tucked himself in to prepare to wake in an hour or so to "find" Tempest and save him.

~ ~ ~

He was walking down a hot dusty street in Helmand province, southern Afghanistan. His SAS unit was stationed at Camp Bastion, a sprawling military installation complete with airfield that had at one time housed almost 10,000 British troops, but now housed about 2,000. They were closing the base soon, and he would be home. Thank God!

Now, however, he was on a special mission that combined his SAS unit with a U.S. Navy SEAL unit in search of a dangerous insurgent believed to be holed up in their area.

Suddenly, sniper fire rang out from the rooftop of a nearby building, and the man next to him fell to the ground, killed instantly by a bullet in the head. "Get down! Get down!" he shouted to the rest of his troops. "Take cover! Anywhere you can find it!" He quickly scrambled to shelter in the doorway of a nearby home that had been long deserted, and searched the streets for the rest of his unit. More shots rang out and bullets raised puffs of dust near his feet. He could see the rest of his men were also pinned down by gunfire, and there didn't seem to be any specific target they could shoot back at. It was time to call in some air support. He located his communication device, and notified Camp Bastion that they were under attack. He provided their coordinates and requested backup and air support, either helicopter or even drone support. They just needed to know where the enemy was so they could take them out.

Eventually, a chopper arrived, and easily dispatched the three or four snipers that had pinned them down. He noticed his best friend, Neil McCauley, sauntering over to him as if he hadn't a care in the world.

"You bloody stupid bugger!" Ian shouted. "Be careful. You don't know for sure if they got them all yet." As soon as the words left his mouth, a shot rang out, and Neil clutched at the gaping wound that had opened his throat.

"No! No! No!" Ian cried. "Neil!" He ran over to Neil's lifeless body as the last of his life blood spilled out on the dusty ground. "My God, no!" For the first time since he had arrived in Afghanistan, Ian cried like a baby. He was still sobbing Neil's name as they dragged him away from the body.

"No!" Ian threw off the covers and sat up in bed as he awoke from his nightmare, the same nightmare that had repeated itself over and over again every night without fail since he returned home from Afghanistan. The doctors kept telling him that it would get better with time, but it had been almost a year, and the nightmare, although occurring less frequently, was still as vivid as ever. He had sought solace in alcohol, but even that didn't prevent the recurrence. Sighing and looking at the clock, he saw it was a little past midnight, and since he wasn't going to go back to sleep anytime soon, Ian decided to go for a walk in the barn. For some reason, the peaceful presence of the horses calmed him like nothing else could, and he could use the serenity. He pulled on a pair of sweatpants and a T-shirt, donned his athletic shoes, and left the house.

Once at the barn, Ian noticed right away that the horses were much more agitated than that usually were at this hour. As he approached the grain room, he noticed there was horse inside, greedily helping himself to the sweet feed. It was Tempest. "Jesus, horse, you're not supposed to be in there!" Ian knew right away this was trouble, and ran immediately back to the house to get Michael.

"Mike! Mike! Wake up!" Ian shook Michael until he finally woke from what appeared to be a very deep sleep.

"What? Ian? What's the matter? Why are you up? Is it another nightmare?"

"Yes. I had a nightmare, but that's not why I'm here. It's Tempest. He's gotten out of his stall, and is eating the grain in the grain room like there's no tomorrow."

Michael's face paled. "Oh my God! I've got to stop him. He'll make himself sick. Come along and help me. I may need another set of hands to get him out of there."

Michael quickly changed into jeans, a T-shirt, and athletic shoes and both he and Ian ran back out to the barn. Sure enough, Tempest was enjoying the sweet feed at an alarming rate. Michael grabbed the stallion's halter from his stall and approached him slowly. "Easy now, boy, you have to come with me. That stuff's bad for you in large quantities, and I don't want you to get a belly ache. That wouldn't be at all pleasant." Instead of trying to put the halter on, Michael looped the lead rope around Tempest's neck and attempted to lead him away from the grain that way. Thankfully, Tempest didn't put up much of a fight, and allowed himself to be led back to his stall.

"Ian, please call the vet and ask him to get over here immediately. I'll check the grain room and see if I can figure out just how much grain he ate before you found him." Ian nodded and moved back toward the house. "By the way, brother, I owe you a debt of gratitude. If you hadn't been here to stop him, Tempest may have eaten all that grain. If he foundered after that it might have been too serious to remedy and we might have had to put him down. You saved his life, Ian."

Ian smiled. This was the first time he could think of that he was thankful for his nightmares.

When Ian entered the house, Jessica was making her way down the staircase, yawning and clearly just awakened. "I heard some commotion. What's going on, Ian? Is everything all right?"

"It's Tempest, Jessica. I have to call the vet right away." Ian found Michael's cell phone, located the vet's number in his contacts, and placed the call. After what must have been several rings, Ian told the vet to come right over. Jessica listened intently as Ian explained to the vet what had apparently happened. "I discovered the stallion in the grain room eating as much grain as he could get." Ian paused, listening to the vet's question. "I don't know exactly how much he ate, but we know he was in his stall when Michael did his night check at 10 PM. I found him at 12:30 AM." Ian paused again then responded. "Fine. We'll see you when you get here. Thank you!"

As she listened to Ian's end of the conversation, Jessica paled in fear. She ran back up the stairs to change into something more suitable, then, once changed, ran out to the stable. Michael was walking Tempest up and down the aisle. The stallion didn't appear to be in any distress, but that didn't mean that everything was all right. Colic or laminitis could develop over time. Laminitis especially, could take hours to develop, as the sugar from the grain made its way through Tempest's system.

Before Jessica could say anything to Michael, his vet, Dr. David McKnight, arrived. Jessica noted that Dr. McKnight was in his mid-forties, medium build, about six feet tall, with light-brown hair that looked a bit tousled, as if he had just gotten out of bed. Jessica smiled to herself. He probably had just gotten out of bed to answer their emergency call. His attitude was one of professional concern as he approached the barn.

Knowing Ian had described what had happened to Tempest when he called, she knew he was prepared to get started with treatment right away. He had brought from his truck some items familiar to Jessica after several years around a number of horses: a stomach tube and funnel. "Michael, how is he? Does he have a fever, or is he showing any signs of colic?" the vet asked.

Michael said, "Nothing, David. I looked in the grain bin, and it appears he may not have had time to eat more than a gallon, but that's still more than he gets as a regular ration."

"Good," the vet said. "I still think it would be a good idea to tube him with mineral oil and Banamine to prevent colic. It will also ensure any toxins produced by the excess sugar don't cause laminitis. Laminitis is a disease of the hoof, caused when internal tissues, called laminae, weaken, and the horses pedal bone detaches from the inside of the hoof. When detached, the pedal bone can turn, and sometimes, it even pushes through the sole. When it pushes through the sole, it's called founder. It's very painful to the horse, and if not treated or if it is severe it can cause permanent lameness. Horses in that situation would have to be put down or face a lifetime of excruciating pain."

"I've heard of horses foundering, but have never experienced it in one of my horses, thank goodness. I do know it can be extremely painful for the horse," Jessica said. "I'm so glad you found him when you did, Ian. You probably saved his life."

Michael also expressed his gratitude to Ian. He looked to Tempest, who was still not exhibiting any signs of distress, but was watching the small group of humans surrounding him with interest. "He isn't going to like this," Michael said. "But we have to do it. Jessica, please help me keep him calm so David can insert the tube, and give him the mineral oil and Banamine."

"Sure. No problem." Jessica approached the stallion, who began to tense as the attention shifted back to him. The vet prepared the mineral oil and Banamine mixture, and as Jessica and Michael talked to the stallion in soft, comforting tones, David slowly and carefully inserted the naso-gastric tube into Tempest's nostril, and guided it down his throat to his stomach. He slowly poured the liquid mixture into the tube so that it would go directly to Tempest's stomach. The stallion's eyes grew rounder, and the whites started showing, but Michael was at his side, soothing him with his voice, and slowly stroking his neck. Jessica held the lead rope and also did her best to speak soothingly to Tempest as the procedure progressed. The stallion calmed and stopped resisting the procedure. When the container holding the oil/Banamine mixture was empty, the doctor slowly withdrew the tube.

"Now, we wait," the vet said. "I recommend you continue to walk him until he passes gas or manure and we know his digestive system is working. Hopefully, we'll know in an hour or so if this treatment worked."

"Thank you, David. I'm so glad you could get here so quickly."

"You're lucky. You were my only emergency tonight." He smiled ruefully. "I should have known that expecting to get a full night's sleep on my on-call night was too good to be true."

Ian started walking Tempest up and down the barn aisles, and the tension that had been infecting the group began to recede. Michael noticed his vet looking at Jessica with curiosity, and realized he may be wondering who she was and why she was here on his farm in the middle of the night. He decided to simplify the explanation, since David didn't need to know every detail of the circumstances surrounding Jessica's presence. "David McKnight, this is Jessica Warren, an American dressage rider here to train with me on this stallion." He looked over at Jessica. "Jessica, David was the vet for the British Olympic team before I persuaded him to follow me here to Surrey."

"Wow. I'm impressed. I had no idea Michael could be that persuasive." Jessica looked over at him and grinned, and he winked in response.

"Actually, my practice wasn't far from here, in Sussex," David said. "I still have many of my previous clients, but I've taken on Michael since we met in London for the Games last year. I haven't regretted my association with him. He treats his horses very well."

David offered his hand, and Jessica clasped his hand warmly. "It's very nice to meet you, Jessica. Michael, as you probably know, is an excellent horseman. I'm sure you'll learn a lot from him while you're here."

"Yes. I'm sure I will," Jessica responded, looking over at Michael. She blushed when Michael met her gaze with warmth and, if she wasn't mistaken, a hint of desire. Where did that come from? Jessica felt her entire body heat under his perusal, and she felt parts of herself stirring that hadn't come alive in quite some time. She cleared her throat, and broke the visual contact by looking back at the vet.

Just as she was about to make a comment, Lionel appeared at the barn door. "What's going on out here? Did I miss something?"

"Lionel, I'm surprised you slept through all the commotion," Michael responded. "Tempest escaped from his stall, and broke into the grain room. He helped himself to about a gallon of sweet feed. Thank God Ian couldn't sleep and wandered out to the barn to check on the horse, and discovered him. We called David and he treated him right away. He's going to be fine."

Lionel looked over at Ian, still walking Tempest up and down the aisle, and ruthlessly stifled the frustration he was feeling that his plan had not worked as he had hoped. "Yes, thank God, indeed." *I can't believe my rotten luck. Now what?* Lionel smiled at the group hoping his expression conveyed relief rather than frustration. "If all is settled, I think I'll go back to bed and see if I can get some sleep. Good night all." Just as Lionel was turning to leave the stable, Ian approached with Tempest. The stallion saw Lionel, immediately turned his rump toward him and farted explosively in his direction. The fart was immediately followed by a stream of loose, wet, and very smelly manure which landed right at Lionel's feet. It was so close, in fact, that some of the wet manure splashed onto Lionel's shoes. The stallion groaned in relief and audibly sighed after losing that intestinal burden, then nudged Ian indicating he was ready to be led back to his stall.

"Well, Lionel," Michael said as he tried without success to stifle his mirth. "It appears that Tempest is trying to tell you something. Do you have any idea what you've done to deserve such noxious treatment?"

Jessica, David and Ian were also trying mightily to remain silent, but snorts of their suppressed giggles filled the stable.

"I do not," Lionel said as he attempted as best he could to retain his dignity, and walked back to the house. He cringed as the trio behind him in the stable burst out in raucous laughter.

Chapter 15

The next day, Michael talked to Tiffany to find out what she might know about why Tempest's stall door was left unlatched, and why the grain room door was left open. "Michael, I swear to you that when I left the barn after feeding dinner last night, the grain room was tightly closed, and Tempest's stall, as well as all the other horses' stall doors, were securely latched."

"Was anyone else out here when you left yesterday, Tiff?"

"No. No one. All the workers leave before I do, and there would have been no reason why any of them would have come back after hours. None."

Michael was stumped. He did check at 10 o'clock that night, and hadn't noticed the grain room open or Tempest's stall unlatched. It was simply too coincidental that only Tempest's stall was unlatched, and that the grain room door was open at the same time. This smacked of an intentional act by someone to injure Tempest, and make it appear as an accident. The perpetrator would have to be someone who knew horses, because few laymen knew that excessive grain could cause a horse serious injury. Michael was troubled. There appeared to be someone intent on sabotaging Michael's, or Jessica's, or both of their chances of success with Tempest. At the very least, it was clear someone meant Tempest harm. That was something he could not tolerate. Unfortunately, all he had was suspicion. There was no clear evidence of tampering or deliberate interference, so he couldn't involve the police. He would have to do his own investigation and would have to take precautions that something like this couldn't happen again. He decided he would sleep in the loft over Tempest's stall for the next few nights, and see if the villain would try to strike again.

That being decided, he went back to the house to tell Jessica what he planned to do. He found her having lunch in the manor dining room. He pulled out a chair and sat at the table across from her to explain his plan.

"What will you do if you actually encounter the person?" Jessica asked. She was more than a little concerned when she heard Michael's plan. If what Michael believed was true, the perpetrator had no difficulty causing an animal harm, and would most likely not hesitate to injure anyone that tried to stand in their way.

"I won't engage the person unless I absolutely have to," Michael replied. "Unless I see that he or she is likely to cause some immediate harm, I'll just keep an eye on them while I call the police."

"I still don't like it," Jessica responded. "Are you sure there isn't any other way?"

"I've looked at this from every angle, and I can't think of anything else. David says that Tempest will be fine to ride again in a couple of days, so this is the best time for the saboteur to try again. If he or she does, I'll be waiting."

Ian had walked into the dining room and heard the last part of the conversation. "If you need someone to spend the night in the barn, Michael, let me do it. I'm out there during the night most evenings anyway, since my nightmares still plague me."

"No, Ian. You need to at least try to get some sleep. Didn't the NHS doctor give you sleeping pills to help you sleep through the night? You should be taking those and getting your rest. Although I do admit that I'm glad you weren't taking them last night. You truly did save Tempest's life."

"I hate those pills," Ian said vehemently. "They knock me out so much that I have trouble waking up the next day. I'm afraid if something happens during the night while I'm on the medication, I'll not be able to wake up and help. What if there's a fire, or one of the horses is injured or colics?"

"Your getting a good night's sleep is more important than anything. Please, for my peace of mind, take the pills at least until the nightmares fade. The doctor did say that eventually they'll recede and not be so vivid, right?"

Ian sighed. "Yes, but she couldn't assure me exactly when that would happen. I'm concerned that I'll get hooked on the sleeping pills if I rely on them for any length of time. The doctor warned me they were addictive."

"Damn it!" Michael said. "There doesn't appear to be any easy answers, but the bottom line here is that this is my responsibility and I will be the one monitoring Tempest. I won't accept any other solution."

Ian and Jessica shared a look of concern, but they also realized by the tone of Michael's voice that he had made up his mind, and there was no changing it.

"All right," Jessica sighed. "We'll back off. But please promise us you'll be careful."

"I promise," Michael said, hoping that neither Jessica nor Ian noticed he crossed his fingers behind his back. He knew that if anyone seriously threatened those dearest to him, including his horses, Michael wouldn't hesitate to do whatever was required to stop them. There could be no other way.

As night approached, Michael gathered his pillow and two large but lightweight blankets and made his way to the stable. Only Ian and Jessica knew he was spending the night in the stable, lying in the hayloft over the main aisle of stalls directly over Tempest's stall so he could watch over the stallion and ensure that whoever had tried to hurt him the night before would be caught if he or she tried again this night.

In the barn, Michael used a large quantity of loose hay in the loft to fashion a bed of sorts in the area just above Tempest's stall. The stallion occasionally looked up with interest, most likely thinking he would be getting a flake or two of hay thrown down to him at any time. Michael located a freshly cleaned winter turnout blanket, and laid it nylon side down against the hay to prevent the stems from poking through and irritating him all night. The inside lining was quilted flannel, and actually very comfortable. He covered himself with the blankets he had brought from the house, and fluffed his pillow. In the loft next to him he had laid a pitchfork. Who knew what he might encounter, and a pitchfork was as good protection as anything. He refused to buy a gun, and he had no experience using a knife. The pitchfork would have to do. After making a final check to ensure all was as it should be, Michael settled in for what expected to be a long, restless night.

Jessica had watched from her bedroom window as Michael made his way into the barn. She noticed he took blankets and a pillow with him, confirming that he planned to spend the entire night in the loft on the lookout for the saboteur to try again. Jessica was not at all comfortable with Michael's plan, but she couldn't see a way to convince him there was a better way. She herself understood that what happened to Tempest last night couldn't have been a coincidence, and she had racked her brain all day trying to come up with a better solution, but to no avail. She sighed and returned to her bed, knowing she wouldn't be able to sleep knowing Michael was potentially in danger.

After an hour of tossing and turning, Jessica looked over at her alarm clock, which showed it was only midnight. *Well, this isn't going to work,* Jessica thought to herself. *Maybe I should go out to the barn and join Michael in his vigil. That way, we could ensure that at least one of us was getting some sleep while the other kept watch. If Michael is there all alone,* she reasoned, *there was a chance he could fall asleep from exhaustion or boredom and miss the saboteur. Not to mention that I owe him an apology for jumping all over him when he tried to help me find help for Hailey. He didn't deserve my bad attitude, and I most likely hurt his feelings by essentially telling him to butt out because it wasn't his business.*

The decision made, Jessica pulled on a pair of lightweight sweatpants, slipped a pair of tennis shoes on over her bare feet, and elected not to change out of her oversized T-shirt that doubled as a night shirt. It definitely covered her, and she would be sleeping some of the time anyway so she might as well be comfortable.

As Jessica left the house, she realized that Michael wouldn't be expecting her, and might mistake her for an intruder. She needed to alert him to her presence without alarming him. She needn't have worried, because as she got closer to the stable, she heard Michael's low voice, speaking softly in the dark. She found him in front of Tempest's stall, stroking his neck, and soothing him. Apparently, Tempest was fretful this evening, possibly still suffering some aftereffects of last night's tubing.

Michael looked up as he heard her approach. "Jess. What are doing out here?"

"I couldn't sleep, and thought you might like some company." Seeing Michael's uncertainty, she pressed on with further explanation. "I feel some responsibility for Tempest's welfare too, you know. I should be here with you watching over him." She approached the stallion and rubbed his forehead. The stallion lowered his head and rumbled his appreciation for the attention.

"I was just thinking about how much is at stake, and what might have happened if we lost Tempest," Michael said. "I'm also trying to figure out who hates me so much that they're willing to seriously injure such a magnificent animal to hurt me." Michael looked so troubled that Jessica reached out to him, and slid her arms around his waist, and pressed her body against him to offer him comfort.

Surprised but pleased, Michael returned the hug, his arms surrounding her in a warm embrace, and Jessica sighed. This felt so right, so wonderful. She had no idea how much she had been longing for the comfort and protection Michael offered. Her heart swelled with emotion.

Michael's hands caressed her back in large, soothing circles, and she lifted her head and saw her longing echoing in Michael's eyes. She stretched up and touched Michael's lips with hers, hoping she hadn't misinterpreted the desire and acceptance she had seen in his eyes. She hadn't.

Michael inhaled her scent, a combination of floral scents mixed with a hint of her own personal spice as he returned her kiss tentatively at first. Jessica parted her lips and teased his mouth with her tongue and Michael moaned with pleasure, allowing her access and deepened the kiss. Their tongues mingled and danced and both reveled in the excitement and heat they were generating. Jessica's arms moved up to encircle Michael's neck, and she ran her fingers tentatively through his thick, soft hair. Such a delicious feeling. Michael broke off the kiss, and his fingers tenderly traced the line of Jessica's jaw. He cupped her chin and tilted her head up to make sure she met his eyes.

"I think I've wanted to do that since I first saw you," Michael said, his eyes darkening with desire. "Are you sure this is what you want, Jess? Because if we go through with this, our relationship will never be the same. I won't be able to see you as just a student or as a competitor for Tempest that I must defeat. To be honest, I don't know exactly where we would go from here, but I'm willing to give it a try if you are."

"Yes, Michael," Jessica replied with a confidence that frankly surprised her. Evidently, she had been considering this possibility for some time, too. Interesting. "I want this just as much as you do."

Michael grinned. "In that case, milady, please proceed upstairs. My *boudoir* awaits." He bowed most formally as he waved his arm to indicate the ladder leading up to the hayloft. Jessica noticed he was purposely mimicking a formal British lord much like the ones she read about in the few romance novels she had read.

Jessica, now faced with the reality of her situation, found herself growing a bit nervous. *Courage, Jess. You know you want this. Just relax and enjoy.* She decided to play along with the game he had started, and assumed the persona of a formal British lady. She stiffened her posture, returned his smile, and affected her best British accent. "Certainly, milord, I look forward to partaking of your hospitality."

Jessica started up the hayloft ladder, giving Michael an excellent view of her perfectly shaped buttocks as she climbed. Michael swallowed past the lump that had developed in his throat. This woman was so beautiful, yet she had no idea how much she affected him. She was physically attractive, yes, but what drew him to her like a moth to a flame was her easy nature, her intelligence, and her honesty. There was no subterfuge with this woman. After his experience with Emma, that meant more to him than he had realized.

Once they both arrived at the loft, she saw the cozy nest he had created for himself with the quilted blanket and covers. Since he had only just left it, as she got closer, she was surrounded by his scent, a combination of sandalwood, spice and a touch of sweetness she couldn't label, but it excited her senses like nothing she had ever experienced before. She kneeled slowly down onto the improvised bed and looked up at Michael. Smiling shyly, she patted the quilting next to her. Michael slowly lowered himself to kneel next to her, and curled his hand around the back of her neck, bringing her mouth to his for a deeply searing kiss. Their tongues clashed in a heated exchange, and Michael used his other hand to slide gently under Jessica's oversized t-shirt. Her heated skin was silky soft and smooth to the touch. He skimmed his hand up over her ribcage to cradle a breast. "No bra?" he teased.

"I was planning to sleep." Jessica blushed.

"I'm not complaining, love." Michael chuckled. "I'm appreciating." His thumb brushed over her nipple, and she gasped at the flash of energy that heated her and generated a pool of warmth in her core. She tingled all over. He changed position to grasp the bottom of her T-shirt with both hands, and slowly lifted it over her head as she raised her arms to ease the way.

"Beautiful, just beautiful." Michael sighed. His eyes trailed slowly over her naked torso, and he gazed with pure admiration at her perfectly formed, pink-tipped breasts. He noticed her nipples had hardened to darker pink points. He couldn't resist taking one in his mouth, and licked, teased and suckled until she moaned in pleasure.

Jessica arched into Michael's mouth, her insides melting in liquid heat at the sensations his caresses were creating. Slowly, after giving equal attention to Jessica's other breast, he slowly made his way lower. He trailed kisses down Jessica's stomach, eliciting shivers of excitement, then reached the waistband of her sweatpants. He started peeling her sweatpants down and noticed Jessica was wearing no panties either.

"My dear girl." Michael grinned up at her. "You're my dream come true."

Jessica laughed as Michael finished pulling down her sweatpants, and quickly removed her shoes as well. She was now completely naked, she noticed, but Michael was still wearing all of his clothes. "Unfair," she said as she reached for the bottom of his T-shirt and ran her hands underneath. "It's your turn to show some skin, milord."

Michael graciously complied, easily stripping off his T-shirt, then standing for a quick removal of his sweatpants and shoes. His burgeoning erection stood tall against his flat, toned belly, occasionally jerking with tension. Jessica's gaze was immediately drawn to his thick, long length, and beckoned him to join her again in their makeshift bed. He immediately complied. He took her again in his arms, and kissed her deeply once again. He urged her to lie back on the soft quilting. This time there was nothing to interrupt as he trailed kisses down Jessica's body until he reached the nest of curls at the junction of her thighs. He only paused a moment to grin up at her shocked expression before his mouth covered her hot, moist folds, and his tongue flicked over her most sensitive spot.

Jessica groaned with pleasure, the sensations so exquisite she nearly couldn't breathe. As Michael worked to stimulate her to greater and greater heights, she realized her hips were rocking in a steady rhythm, and Michael was holding her buttocks to keep her in place for easy access. Suddenly, the tension that had been building inside of her exploded in a burst of energy and sensation, her insides throbbing with the rhythm. As her body continued to throb, his mouth played her body like a musical instrument built only for him.

When the sensations finally ebbed, Jessica fell back on the blanket completely drained, pleasantly fuzzy. "Oh. My. God," she said.

"I aim to please," Michael replied with a satisfied smile.

Jessica noticed, however, that his body was till taut with unfulfilled desire. She reached for his penis, hard and hot, but so soft to the touch, and gently stroked.

Michael groaned. "God, Jess. That feels so good."

Jessica licked her lips sensuously, and moved to take him in her mouth, thinking that turnabout was fair play.

Michael noticed her intent, and gently pushed her back to the blanket. "Not this time, love. I want to be inside you."

Jessica would have been happy to oblige, because the thought of him filling her with his long, hard, heat was very exciting. However, there were risks. "I would love that, Michael. Do you have any protection?"

Damn! "No, sweetheart, I don't. Not here anyway. I obviously hadn't planned on a tryst in the hay when I came out here earlier." Jessica could tell Michael was frustrated. She knew Michael wanted to consummate their relationship, and she was shocked when she realized how strongly she shared his primitive desire to be possessed completely, wanting him to make her his, to claim her physically, to literally plant his seed in her.

"Where are you in your cycle?" he asked, desperate that it be safe to complete their union.

"Um, I think it's okay," Jessica tried to clear her muddled brain enough to make some quick math calculations and tried to visualize a calendar in her head. It would be close, but they would probably be safe. She crossed her fingers. There was no way in this moment that she would say no. "Yes, I'm sure it will be okay." She told him.

Anxious to believe her, Michael proceeded. He lowered himself over Jessica, covering her face with kisses, at first light and playful, then when he reached her mouth, deeper and more sensual, generating even more heat than before. Jessica raked her fingers through Michael's hair, as he trailed lower to suckle her breasts again until she was writhing with need underneath him. "I think you're ready for me now, love," He said. He nudged her thighs with his knees, and she opened to him without hesitation. He knew he needed to go slow, since he had no idea when, if ever, Jessica had last had a lover. Jessica made his job more difficult by arching her hips into him, begging him to take her and make her his own.

"Easy, Jess. I want to make this good for you, so I'm trying to take it slow."

"No, Michael, not slow. I want you now," Jessica demanded. "It's fine. I'm ready. Please, Michael, please." She moved her hands lower on his back and gripped his buttocks to emphasize her need, and he relented. Grateful for her permission, he positioned himself at her entrance and thrust inside her.

She gasped with the initial shock of his entry, then moaned in pleasure. Assured that everything was all right, he began to stroke in and out and she wrapped her legs and arms around him, holding him to her as if she would never let go. "Yes! Yes. Just like that." Although Jessica was whispering, he understood her need, and obeyed her urging to continue. He could feel her internal muscles tightening, and knew she was close to peaking again. "Let's come together, love," he whispered. "Come with me now." His stokes became faster as he felt his own release nearing, and he whispered to her again. "Let go, love. Trust me. Let me have you." At just that moment, he felt her cry out as she started convulsing around him, and he let go, emptying himself deep insider her. When he could no longer feel her pulsing around him, he withdrew slowly and collapsed to his back, taking her with him. She snuggled against him with a sigh and laid a hand on his chest, just over his heart. Michael pressed a kiss to her temple and pushed her hair away from her face and back behind her ear. *You're mine. All mine.* Those were his last thoughts as he tucked her exhausted and satisfied body next to him and covered them with warm, soft blankets. They both fell into a deep, comfortable sleep.

Michael slowly awakened to the sound of birds chirping and of horses stirring in their stalls, most likely hungry for their morning meal. The sun was beginning to peek over the eastern horizon, and he felt the warm presence of a beautiful woman clinging to him, their legs entwined intimately together. The pungent but sweet smell of crushed hay surrounded him, mixed with Jessica's sweet scent, and the musky smell of their lovemaking and he felt himself becoming more aroused as he awakened from the best sleep he had experienced in months. Unfortunately, the next sound Michael heard was his brother, Ian, shouting at the top of his lungs. "Good morning, Tiffany! How are you this fine day?" Michael strained to hear Tiffany's response as he tried to move from his cozy nest only to find his arm pinned underneath Jessica's still sleeping head.

"Wake up, sweetheart," Michael whispered gently in her ear. "We're about to be discovered, so unless you want Tiffany to find us here naked, you have to go."

Jessica's eyes flew open. "Oh, shit!" She went instantly from pleasantly lazy to wide-awake, her heart pounding as she tried to quickly disentangle herself from Michael without causing bodily harm and bolted upright to start frantically searching for her clothes.

Michael couldn't help grinning at her behavior. Knowing that he wasn't helping, and realizing her distress was real, he tried to reassure her. "There's no need to panic, love. I have a feeling Ian took one of his midnight walks last night and heard us up here in the loft. My guess is he's doing his best to cover for us while we make ourselves presentable."

"Oh my God, Michael," Jessica said, blushing a deep shade of red. "Do you really think Ian heard us? That he knows what we did last night?" When Michael's grin widened in response to her question, she groaned. "I'm so embarrassed. What will he think?"

Michael pulled on his sweat pants and considered. The playfulness in his voice was gone. He wanted to be sure Jessica understood he was serious. "He'll be glad I'm happy, and that you're the woman I've chosen to be intimate with after a long period of enforced celibacy," Michael responded honestly. "He's been worried about me lately, and he actually encouraged me to take our relationship to a more serious level. He likes you, Jessica. He likes you a lot." *So do I.*

Jessica couldn't meet Michael's gaze. She had a lot to think about. She definitely heard the tone of Michael's voice, and the underlying message he was conveying. There was obviously more to this encounter in Michael's view than a casual one-night stand. Was that what she wanted? She definitely cared for Michael, probably more than she should, given her past and the secret she held inside. A secret that could cause him to reject her in disgust and never want to see her again. She finished dressing, stood up, and slipped her shoes on as Michael approached.

He extended his hand to her, and she clasped it. He pulled her into his embrace, and held her in his arms, stroking her back soothingly, until Ian's voice once again intruded. This time he was just at the top of the ladder to the hayloft. "There you are, Michael," he said, overly loudly to Michael's way of thinking, but he knew the volume was for Tiffany's benefit.

Jessica moved away from Michael as Ian climbed from the ladder into the loft and stood there grinning from ear to ear. He winked at them and motioned to Jessica that there was another ladder at the opposite end of the barn that would take her out of the hayloft. If she left from that direction, she could make it back to the house, with no one the wiser that she had ever been in the loft with Michael. Jessica smiled her thanks at Ian, who took an exaggerated bow, then she made her way out.

"So, brother." Ian couldn't help but give his big brother some grief over being discovered in a compromising position. "You're not providing me a very good example. Shagging in the hayloft no less." Michael had the grace to look sheepish, then Ian turned serious. "Good show, man! Honestly, I'm proud of you, Michael. Jessica's a really great girl."

"She is, isn't she?" Michael smiled self-consciously. Then he also got serious. "Ian, I've never felt like this about any woman, even Emma. It bloody frightens me to death."

What if I'm wrong about her? What if she betrays me like Emma did? I don't think I could survive the pain. Michael kept those thoughts to himself, because his heart told him the Jessica was nothing like Emma, and that he could trust her with his heart.

"Welcome to real life, brother." Ian wrapped his arm around Michael's shoulders and squeezed him hard. "I wish I had the courage to join you."

"You'll get there, Ian. I have faith." He moved to embrace his brother, and that's how Tiffany found them when she climbed up the ladder to see what was going on.

After assuring Tiffany that the night had been uneventful and checking on Tempest, who appeared to be nearly back to normal, Michael went to the house to get some breakfast and find Jessica. He found her in the kitchen, making some scrambled eggs and bacon. "It looks like you're making enough for two, or are you that hungry after our exertions last night?" He grinned. She threw a kitchen towel at him, but was trying without success to suppress a grin of her own.

"I assumed you would be as hungry as I am, so I cooked enough for both of us." Once the food was ready and the coffee brewed, she served Michael then herself and they settled in to eat. As she sipped her hot coffee, Jessica let her mind wander to what had happened in the hayloft last night. Now, in the light of day, she wondered how her relationship with Michael would change now that they had become lovers. How would she be able to compete with him for Tempest? Most importantly, how did she feel about him? One thing was certain: she had never felt like this about anyone. True, her experience with men was limited to the one guy from high school that she had thought she would marry, but never in her relationship with Mark had she felt this soul-deep connection, that feeling that this man was her other half, and she would be lost if he wasn't in her life. Michael must have sensed her thoughts, because at just that moment, he reached across the table and took her hand in his, squeezing it gently in reassurance.

"It'll be all right," he said calmly. "I'm in uncertain territory as well, but something deep inside me tells me this is right."

Jessica sighed, and rubbed her thumb across the back of his hand. He was right. She knew in her heart that this relationship was different, deeper, than anything she had ever experienced before. It wasn't just the physical attraction, no, it was so much more than that. She leaned across the table and met Michael halfway as they shared a brief, tender kiss.

The moment was interrupted when Jessica's cell phone rang. Jessica looked to see who was calling, tempted to send the caller to voicemail and continue her time alone with Michael, but it was Hailey calling. She showed Michael the caller ID, and he nodded his understanding. As Jessica answered, Michael started cleaning up.

"Hey, sis," Jessica said. "I'm sorry I didn't call you at our regular time. Is everything all right?"

"Everything's great," Hailey answered. "Blake McMillan's secretary. Oops, I mean his 'personal assistant'"—Jessica could hear the air quotes in Hailey's voice—"called me, and he's arranged for both Liz and me to fly over there with him late next week."

"Liz is coming too?" Jessica couldn't hide her surprise at the news. "I thought she was stuck there until her custody suit was finished."

"I don't know the details, Jess, but I'm pretty sure the woman said both Liz and I would be on the jet. Maybe you should call Liz and get the story from her."

"I definitely will." Jessica was certainly puzzled. When she had called Liz to let her know what had happened to Tempest, she hadn't mentioned anything about her custody case being settled or that she planned to travel back to England. Strange.

At that very moment, Liz was making last-minute arrangements with her sister Cynthia to split Amy's time equally with Rick while Liz was away in the UK. To everyone's surprise, including Rick's attorney, Rick had withdrawn his custody suit and sat down with Liz and her attorney to draw up a temporary custody arrangement so that he could have more time with Amy while Liz was out of the country without changing their long term shared custody arrangement. Amy had been overjoyed that her parents were no longer fighting, and Liz suspected she had played more of a role in changing Rick's mind than she was letting on. No matter, it was done, and everyone was happy. Liz could now switch her focus to Jessica and her training on Tempest.

Under Michael's tutelage, Jessica was making great strides in mastering the big stallion. As she viewed video after video of her training sessions, Liz was mightily impressed with Michael's skill as a trainer, and quite frankly felt a bit unneeded at this point. She reminded herself that Michael was still the competition, and that although she didn't see video of Michael's rides like she had of Jess, Michael had to be making progress with the stallion as well.

Liz also had to acknowledge that she really missed being there in person, and definitely wanted to have a chance to ride Tempest herself. He was such a magnificent animal, and with the right rider, could easily be a world and Olympic champion. Liz knew she could be that rider. *Stop dreaming, Liz. That's not your life now. You have other responsibilities.* Liz sighed. Competitive riding wasn't in her future, as much as she might want it. She had too many responsibilities between the therapeutic riding business and her daughter. There just wasn't the time to devote to her riding that she would need to compete at the highest levels. She, of anyone, knew that. Her job now was to coach Jess to success, and she was determined to do just that.

Chapter 16

Blake McMillan was making last minute arrangements for his trip to the UK, ostensibly for business, but in reality to finally make his move on Jessica and make her his. He had been avidly watching the videos his sister Charlotte provided him of Jessica riding Tempest and what he saw confirmed that this woman was exactly what he wanted. Blake knew nothing of dressage, but watched Jessica's training sessions in open admiration. Her lithe, athletic body, especially those long, beautiful legs, entranced him more than any woman had in recent memory. He could easily imagine her riding him with the same fluid, athletic grace, her hips undulating over him, draining him of every last—he stopped in his reflection to adjust his pants, which had suddenly become much tighter. God, he had to get over there, and soon.

~ ~ ~

It had been three days since Tempest's near disaster, and David declared him ready for riding. Michael allowed Jessica to take the first day, and they were back to their routine in no time. Although their personal relationship had changed, both Jessica and Michael worked hard to maintain a professional demeanor when they rode, although Jessica was now openly spending time watching Michael's training sessions, even going so far as to occasionally offer advice and observations.

Michael was finding Jessica's active participation in his sessions a joy, and he appreciated the extent of her knowledge and expertise. She also had a very good eye for finding subtleties in his approach to Tempest that enhanced even his own experienced approach. It seemed amazing to him, but it felt as though their physical relationship enhanced their ability to communicate on all levels. It was a heady feeling. He knew he had never had this kind of connection with Emma.

The depth of his feelings for Jessica frightened him in its intensity. Truly, they had only been together as a couple for a matter of days, but it felt as though he had known her forever. In addition, his desire for her had only escalated since their first encounter. It had been impossible to stay away from her after their tryst in the loft, and the couple had, by mutual agreement, been meeting in their love nest in the hayloft every night since, ostensibly to keep watch for Tempest's saboteur. After their first night, Michael made sure to bring protection, so there was no more worry about an accidental pregnancy, which neither of them wanted or needed right now.

Michael reflected on the past few days spent with Jessica, and couldn't believe how happy he was. Even Ian was encouraging him to make the relationship more permanent, but there were still so many things up in the air. Michael also had to admit that in his training sessions with Jessica, she had demonstrated a reluctance to push Tempest beyond his comfort zone and elevate his performance to get the brilliance he was capable of. As a pair, Jessica and Tempest had fallen into a level of performance that got the job done, but lacked the fire necessary to compete and win at the international level. The problem was that Michael knew Tempest could perform at that level. He had asked for it and gotten it a number of times. He also understood that Jessica was probably not even aware that she was holding back. When he attempted to communicate this to Jessica in their sessions, she subtly but stubbornly resisted doing anything that might aggravate Tempest.

He understood that always in the back of Jessica's mind was the fear that if she were injured, or worse killed, her sister Hailey would be all alone in the world, and there was no way she would risk that. He admired her so much for her dedication and support of her sister. It had to have been difficult to survive the emotional shock of losing both parents in an instant then to take complete responsibility for her sister at only twenty-one years of age, not to mention dealing with her sudden disability. It took a very special person to take on that challenge and do it as well as Jessica had. It was one of the things he most admired, and yes, loved about her.

Unfortunately, her reticence about pushing Tempest to the point that he might offer resistance before giving in made it less likely that she would win Tempest for herself. Michael tortured himself with the possibility that that might happen. How would she react if he won the competition for Tempest? Would she be hurt if he won? Then there was also the realization that once the competition was over, win or lose Jessica would be leaving to go back home to Ohio. Once that happened, he knew her absence would leave a gaping hole in his existence. How could they keep their relationship alive? Finally, he couldn't avoid the fear that something unexpected might happen to ruin everything. Hadn't he felt the same way with Emma, who then turned around and betrayed him with another?

Chapter 17

Lionel stood outside of Rocky's stall and studied the gelding. Generally, Rocky's body didn't reveal any visible scars, but the scars he did have were telling. The fact that he was so defensive of his stall indicated to Lionel that someone had abused him while he was in the stall. The abuse could take many forms, but whatever the abuser had done had left its mark on the gelding. The nature of the horse's defense mechanisms— threatening to bite or kick anyone invading his space—indicated the abuse was severe. It took a monumental effort to suppress the rage that surged within him as he contemplated what some human must have done to this horse to cause this behavior. He, of all people, knew what damage abuse, both visible and invisible, could cause.

Lionel had known from a relatively early age that he was different from other boys. He had no interest in playing football or rugby but had a love of horses that transcended any other aspect of his life. In his early and mid-teens, he found himself being attracted to a couple of the other boys in his class, and was drawn to watching gay male pornography on his computer. Unfortunately, Lionel's father had caught him watching online porn and erupted.

His father was a dockworker at the Shoreham Port in Brighton, and refused to accept that his son was gay. He frequently abused him in a cynical attempt to "toughen him up" which only drove Lionel further away. It was after one of these beatings that Lionel rode his bike to the Brighton race track, to be close to the horses and to escape his abusive home. It was his love of horses, and the miracle of love that horses brought to him in the guise of Nigel Crawford, that ultimately saved his life. Lionel knew from experience that first and foremost he needed to get past the rage, because if this sensitive animal sensed rage, he would react in fear, and that would ruin any efforts Lionel needed to make to gain Rocky's trust.

As soon as he knew he would be working with Rocky, Lionel arranged with Michael's barn staff that he be the only person to feed Rocky and the only person to clean his stall, and handle him for turn-out and the like. It was necessary that he build a relationship with the horse, and that the interactions he had with him would only be positive. He decided in Rocky's case, that he would start by grooming the horse to find out exactly how difficult he would be to handle, and which parts of his body he was overly sensitive about. In this way, he might be able to deduce how exactly Rocky had been abused by his previous owners. It had now been two days since Lionel had taken over Rocky's care, and he noticed that Rocky now perked up a bit when he saw Lionel, which was a major improvement. When Michael had first introduced Lionel to Rocky, the horse was practically non-responsive to anyone, and had no interest in the world outside of his stall.

Today, Lionel decided to try to take him out of his stall for the first time, and attempt to groom Rocky. Armed with some apple slices and carrot pieces for rewards, Lionel approached Rocky, led him out of his stall down the aisle then out of the barn to Michael's round pen, which was situated between the barn and the turnout pastures. Once in the round pen, Lionel removed the lead rope, and allowed Rocky free run of the round pen without any restraint. The gelding looked only marginally interested in his surroundings, but did look to Lionel as if to ask for permission to wander. Lionel stood completely still and allowed Rocky to decide for himself what he wanted to do. Eventually, Rocky's innate curiosity overcame his fear, and he ambled slowly around the pen, sniffing the ground and the rails. Lionel smiled to himself. This was progress.

Lionel had left a tote with grooming tools in it near the round pen, so he went over and retrieved a curry comb and slowly approached Rocky speaking to him in low-pitched, soothing voice. Rocky looked at Lionel with some suspicion, but allowed Lionel to gradually apply the curry comb lightly all over his body, but moved away when Lionel tried to use the curry in his belly area. This indicated to Lionel that Rocky had most likely been whipped or kicked in the belly by an abuser, and was trying to protect that area from additional harm. Lionel slowly and gradually tried to move the curry to the more objectionable areas, rewarding Rocky with a carrot or apple when he allowed more freedom of movement, until all areas were covered. Lionel put away the curry and tried to cover the same area with a soft bristled brush and was successful, but ran into a new roadblock when he attempted to pick up Rocky's feet for cleaning. Rocky's reaction to that attempt was violent and fearful, and Lionel was forced to stop without making more progress. He closed their session with another pass of the brush over Rocky's entire body and rewarded him with more treats, so that Rocky wouldn't remember the negative reaction as his last experience in the round pen.

While Lionel worked with Rocky, Michael rode his prospects, then after he finished putting his last horse of the day in his stall, he found Jessica surreptitiously watching Lionel work. She signaled Michael to silence, and motioned to him to join her. It appeared that Lionel was just finishing his session, so Jessica turned to Michael, and the pair walked down the aisle toward the house.

"It looks like he's making progress with Rocky," Jessica said. "Does he have a lot of experience with abused horses?"

"Actually, he does," Michael said. "Lionel makes his living rehabilitating off-the-track thoroughbreds for pleasure riding, either hunt, dressage, or eventing. He is very good at it. A few of the horses he gets from the race track have been abused. There are still some grooms and track staff that are intimidated by the horses, and the only way they know to counter their fear is to bully the horses and make the horses afraid of them. It's a sad state of affairs, but unfortunately still occurs more than one would like, especially on the lower tier tracks."

"How tragic," Jessica responded. "I don't have much experience with the race tracks in America, but my guess is that the same situation occurs there too."

Michael nodded, then decided to change the subject to a more pleasant topic. "I thought I'd take you to dinner at my favorite pub in Guildford, The Golden Hart. Are you interested?"

Jessica smiled. "Sure. I'm game. What time do you want to leave?"

Just at that moment, Lionel called out to them from the barn. "Hey, you two. What are your plans for dinner? I'm starved."

Michael and Jessica exchanged a pained look, but Michael turned around and called back, "We're going to The Golden Hart. We'll be leaving in an hour. Can you be ready?"

"Certainly," Lionel responded. "Don't leave without me."

"Don't tempt me," Michael murmured under his breath, but loud enough for Jessica to hear. She smiled in response. She also would have liked to have a meal alone with Michael, since Lionel made certain to join them for breakfast, lunch, and dinner most days.

"Actually," Lionel said, "I have to go back to my farm for a bit to check on things. Can I meet you at the restaurant?"

Michael smiled, then surreptitiously winked at Jessica. "Yes, of course. That would be fine. See you there."

As the entered the Golden Hart, the hostess beamed at him. "Michael, it is so good to see you again."

"Hello, Rachel," he flashed her one of what Jessica called his "movie star smiles" at the woman, who blushed and hurried to find them a table.

"Rachel, eh?" Jessica whispered to him, feeling pangs of jealousy she couldn't suppress.

"I've been coming here for dinner ever since I bought the yard. She's worked here forever," Michael said. He looked at Jessica curiously, not understanding why she sounded so annoyed. When Jessica took his hand in hers quite obviously, Michael finally understood, and grinned to himself. Recognizing Jessica's sudden possessiveness as a sign of jealousy, he was tempted to tease her, but elected not to. Rachel might get the wrong idea, and he didn't want two women mad at him. One was definitely enough.

"How is Ian?" Rachel asked.

"He's doing all right, considering everything he's been through lately." Michael replied. He hoped Rachel would leave it at that. He didn't want to get into any specifics with Rachel. The local community had supported them when the news of Ian's arrest became public, but he wasn't eager to share more details with the public at large.

"Tell him we're thinking about him," Rachel responded.

"I certainly will, and thank you," Michael replied.

After Michael suggested some of his favorite items on the menu, the trio ordered their meals. After the waitress left them, there was a bit of an awkward silence. Jessica decided to make an attempt to break the ice.

"Lionel, I hope you don't mind," Jessica said, "but I watched you work with Rocky for a while today, and I was impressed with the progress you've made with him in just a few days."

"Thank you, Jessica." Lionel smiled. "Actually, Rocky seems to be a very willing pupil, and open to my attempts to connect with him. That tells me that the abuse he received was most likely short-lived, and that I can move to the next stage of re-training. I've decided to use Michael's round pen to attempt Monty Roberts' Join Up method of training."

"Oh, yes. I've heard of that," Jessica said. "I've actually seen Monty Roberts do a demonstration at the Ohio Equine Affaire a couple of years ago. He is very good."

"Her Majesty the Queen is much taken with Mr. Roberts," Lionel replied. "Nigel and I saw a demonstration he put on in London at the Queen's invitation several years ago, and we decided to incorporate his methods in our training program. It seems to work wonders with all types of horses."

"Who is Nigel?" Jessica asked.

Lionel suddenly looked stricken and avoided Jessica's gaze, focusing instead on his hands tightly folded in front of him on the table.

When it became clear that Lionel wasn't going to answer, Michael intervened. "Nigel was Lionel's partner in his horse training business. I believe Nigel passed away less than a year ago."

"Yes, that's right, Michael.," Lionel said. It was clear that he was still anguished over the loss.

"I'm so sorry, Lionel," Jessica said. "I didn't mean to remind you of your loss. Please forgive me."

"It's all right, Jessica," Lionel attempted a reassuring smile. "You didn't know. I'm trying to recover and go on as Nigel would have wanted, but I still sometimes have a hard time believing he's really gone."

At that moment, their server brought their food, and the three spent the rest of their time commenting on the quality of the food, and the pleasant atmosphere, all making a concerted effort to avoid any more depressing subjects.

On their way back from the restaurant, Jessica reflected on their conversation. She very much regretted causing Lionel to relive a painful memory when she asked him about Nigel.

Michael noticed that Jessica was staring out of the car window, but her focus was elsewhere. "What's troubling you, Jess?"

She turned to look at him and smiled reassuringly. "It's nothing, really," Jessica replied. "I was just thinking about Lionel and Nigel. They must have been very close for Lionel to feel Nigel's loss so strongly."

"From what I saw of them together, they were. I wasn't around Lionel when he and Nigel met, but what I know is that Nigel Crawford had a business rehabilitating race horses for pleasure riding, and he saw Lionel while on one of his buying trips to the track. Nigel noticed right away how good Lionel was with the most difficult horses, and he asked Lionel if he was interested in leaving the track to work for him. Lionel was eager to leave the track and accepted.

"From all accounts, Nigel was a good man, and loved Lionel very much. I know from seeing them together that Lionel returned that love. Lionel and Nigel lived happily together at Nigel's farm in Hickstead, near the All England Jumping Course. Nigel had selected this location years before because many of the thoroughbreds Nigel re-trained were suitable for careers as hunter/jumpers.

"Nigel realized early in their working relationship that Lionel intuitively knew what each individual horse needed in the way of rehabilitation, and was highly successful in matching the horses he trained with the right riders so they could both be successful. Due in large part to Lionel's talents, Nigel's business thrived.

"Nigel also learned that Lionel was a very good rider. Although Lionel was a very good hunter/jumper rider, Nigel believed Lionel would excel most at dressage.

Nigel encouraged Lionel to focus his riding and training in dressage. One of the thoroughbreds Lionel was training showed an incredible talent for dressage. He was a 5-year-old gelding named Accolade.

Lionel and Accolade were a perfect match, and Nigel noticed the affinity the pair had for each other. Accolade would do anything for Lionel, and Lionel's talented riding brought out the gelding's best. In appreciation for all that Lionel had done for him, Nigel gave Lionel Accolade for his own, and paid for him to compete at regional, and then national shows. Ultimately, the two were successful in international dressage competitions. In fact, Lionel and Accolade scored in the top three in several European competitions. While competing, Lionel frequently competed against me and Romeo. Ultimately, we found ourselves competing against each other for a spot on the British Olympic team. It was then that our friendship was challenged."

"What happened?" Michael now had Jessica's complete attention.

Michael continued, suddenly uncomfortable with the direction the conversation had taken. Although his attention never left the road in front of them, Jessica could tell that he was mentally replaying what had happened, and that he didn't relish reliving those events, but he told her, with as much detail as he could remember, what happened at the Olympic trials, and about his subsequent confrontation with Lionel at Nigel's funeral. "I'm surprised Lionel is still speaking to you, let alone maintaining your friendship after what he probably saw as your betrayal at the trials." Jessica paused then said, "The death of his partner after a very public disgrace at the Trials would have pushed many people over the edge. Yet he seems fine. It was only when Nigel's name came up in our conversation that he showed any sign of emotion. Do you think he's really all right?"

Michael had to admit that what Jessica was saying made sense. "I don't know. Two weeks after Nigel's funeral, Lionel contacted me out of the blue and told me he had been thinking, and had decided he was willing to forgive and forget. I confess that I was surprised he was so forgiving so soon after the events, but I chalked it up to our long-term friendship, and that he understood that I did what I thought I had to do."

"Do you think he's the one behind the attempt to injure Tempest?" Jessica asked. "It would be a sort of revenge if he ruined your chances for success."

"I honestly don't think him capable of deliberately injuring a horse," Michael replied. "It just isn't in him to go there."

Jessica sighed. "All right, if you say so. You obviously know him better than I do."

They approached Michael's home, and he parked the car. The evening had been so pleasant that Jessica didn't want to leave Michael yet. Apparently Michael felt the same, because immediately after exiting the car, he quietly suggested that they meet in the hayloft after she'd had a chance to change into more comfortable clothes. Jessica eagerly agreed. It didn't take long for Jessica to change, and she practically ran to the barn in anticipation of another glorious night in Michael's arms. He was already waiting for her when she made it to the top of the ladder.

Later that night, as Jessica lay cuddled against Michael after a slow, languorous session of lovemaking that left them both sated and deliciously drowsy, Michael realized that he was falling in love with Jessica and that if he wanted to take their relationship any further, Jessica needed to know about Emma, and his perspective about how their relationship had fallen apart. He mentally braced himself to relive that painful period in his life.

Jessica seemed to sense the change in his mood, because she immediately looked up at him. "What's wrong, Michael?"

Michael kissed her gently. "Jess, I care about you very much, but it's really difficult for me to trust my heart to someone after what happened between Emma and me last year. I think it's necessary to tell you what happened so you can understand where I'm coming from, and I hope you understand that my reluctance about deepening our relationship says more about me than it does about you."

"Michael, you don't have to explain if it's painful for you."

"Yes, I do." Michael took a deep breath and started. "Before the Olympic Games, Emma and I believed we were truly in love. We shared the same vision for a future together. For me, a career competing in and training dressage and eventually owning my own training yard. For her, working on the support staff for a major London law firm. It wasn't until after my success in the Olympic Games that she appeared to change. She loved sharing the spotlight that shone on me as Olympic champion, and she thrived attending all the parties and fetes that resulted from my success. I was actually quite surprised that she loved the limelight so much. I, quite frankly, hated it and longed to be back on the farm I purchased in the country.

"After I lost Romeo and the Olympic glory faded, she became more distant, and started going to parties with some of the people she met during our time in the spotlight. I just wasn't interested in those things, so I didn't always accompany her to those events. Then, out of nowhere, Emma started accusing me of cheating on her. I was required to travel extensively to do clinics and training sessions, which paid very well, and Emma was somehow convinced I was using those trips as opportunities to be unfaithful. That couldn't have been further from the truth. I swore to her that

I was faithful to her, and tried a thousand ways to convince her I loved her and only her, but she didn't believe me. She finally broke off the engagement. Very soon thereafter, she started dating a famous footballer. I see them frequently in the gossip columns and tabloids. I must assume that she preferred to be with someone who was rich and famous than a has-been dressage rider."

Jessica's heart wrenched at the pain Michael must have felt at the callous way Emma had treated him. She reached up and cradled Michael's jaw in her hand. "I'm so sorry, Michael. You had no way of knowing that Emma was going to change like that. None of this was your fault. Thank you for telling me this. I know it had to be difficult for you." She gently pulled his head down to her, and brushed her lips over his in a gentle kiss, knowing that just the fact that Michael had trusted her to share his most painful experience with her confirmed that he did, indeed, care for her very much, in fact, she was fairly certain that he loved her.

The realization that Michael might love her frightened Jessica. Her experience with men was limited, certainly, but she knew her feelings for Michael went deeper than just their physical relationship. She was slowly falling in love with him, but she didn't know for certain that Michael returned her love. He said all the right things, of course, but he had been with many women. Maybe he told them the same things. All she knew was that she ached to be with him when they weren't together, and she felt herself glow with happiness when they were together. She dreaded the day that the competition would be over, and she would have to go back to Ohio and leave Michael here, an ocean away.

It took all of her strength to force her thoughts back to the present, and she vowed to enjoy every minute of her time with Michael, because it was precious to her. However, the thought that was constantly in the back of her mind, potentially destroying what she had with Michael, persisted. What if he found out about her role in her parents' death? Would he be able to love her then? Did she have the courage to tell him? She pushed those thoughts from her head. Once the competition for Tempest was over, then she would tell him. Until then, she resolved to enjoy herself and hope their relationship would survive her dangerous secret.

Chapter 18

The day finally arrived for Blake McMillan, Hailey and Liz to arrive from the States. As Jessica understood things, Blake had arranged for a limousine to meet his party at the airport, then transport them to Michael's training yard. Michael had arranged for two additional bedrooms in the house to be cleaned and aired, and ready for his guests. Liz would be given the room she had occupied originally; Blake would be further down the hall. Michael had arranged for one of the manor house's former parlor rooms on the ground floor to be converted to a bedroom for Hailey so that she wouldn't have to negotiate stairs every day and to make it easier for her to get around in general. Jessica was grateful for his consideration, and gratified to know that he had taken the time and effort to make Hailey's stay as comfortable as possible.

Jessica fought an attack of nerves, as she paced the manor entryway waiting for the limousine to arrive. Michael took note of Jessica's apparent distress and tried to ease her nerves.

"Calm down, Jess," Michael soothed. "Blake is just a guy. He may have a very high opinion of himself because he's worth a lot of money, but ultimately, he's just like you and me."

"You don't understand, Michael," Jessica responded with a touch of annoyance in her voice. "This 'guy' controls my destiny. He holds my future in his hands. If he decides I'm not worthy to receive the gift of Tempest, he can give him to someone else on the US Equestrian Team without a qualm. His commitment is to the Team, not to me personally. While he's here, I have to impress him enough that he still is willing to buy Tempest for me."

Michael understood her concern, but there was little he could do to assuage her fears. Blake McMillan was a wild card. He didn't know the man, and none of his contacts on the British Equestrian Team knew anything about him either. Apparently, he was new to the equestrian world, and an unknown quantity. Michael vowed he would, to the extent he could, as Jessica's interim trainer, portray Jessica as the talented rider he knew her to be, and hope for the best. He was confident he could do just that, if McMillan was willing to pay attention. In the past two weeks, even with the brief time out required by Tempest's near-colic episode, Jessica's riding of Tempest had improved tremendously. She no longer appeared to be intimidated by his sporadic naughtiness, and didn't let the stallion bully her as he had the first time she rode him. Michael was also interested to see what Liz's reaction would be to seeing Jessica perform on Tempest in person rather than by video. He expected her to be impressed as well.

Just then, a long, black limousine pulled into the drive. "They're here," Jessica said with a mixture of excitement and trepidation. She looked to Michael, reached for his hand. "Let's go out and welcome them." Michael took her hand, squeezed it, and continued to hold it as they walked out the front door to greet the newest arrivals to Stafford Oaks Farm.

The chauffeur had already exited the limo and was opening the rear door closest to Michael and Jessica. Liz emerged first, smiling, and was quickly followed by Hailey, who struggled a bit with her prosthetic legs as she exited the vehicle, but righted herself quickly and stepped out, also sporting a big smile.

Jessica dropped Michael's hand and ran to Hailey, embracing her with a big hug. "Hey, sis, I'm so glad to see you. I missed you so much." Jessica's voice broke, and she couldn't stop the tears that had started running down her face upon seeing her beloved sister.

"Don't cry, Jess." Hailey was tearing up a bit herself. "Everything's great. Blake made the trip really easy. He had a car pick Liz and me up at home, then had us driven directly to the tarmac, so all we had to do was climb up the steps into the plane. His assistants took care of our luggage, and any other details. My wheelchair is in the trunk." Michael had walked up behind Jessica, and extended his hand to Hailey in greeting.

"Hello, Hailey, I'm Michael. It's great to finally meet you in person." He smiled and put his other arm around Jessica just as Blake McMillan was exiting the limo on the other side.

Hailey blushed and shook Michael's hand. "Hi, Michael. I'm glad to meet you in person too. I've got to say that you're even more handsome in person than you are via Skype."

Michael wasn't quite sure how to respond to that comment, so he quickly shifted his attention to Liz. "Liz, it's good to see you again. I trust your legal matters are taken care of, at least for the time being?"

"Yes, Michael," Liz responded. "Everything seems to be all right. Rick has conveniently withdrawn his custody suit, and Amy is safely ensconced with my sister Cynthia while I'm here working with Jess." She sighed. "At least for the time being, all is well." While Liz and Michael were talking, and Jessica and Hailey were catching up, Blake walked around the vehicle and supervised the driver unloading all of their luggage, paid him, including a tip that made the man's eyes pop wide open, then saw him on his way. He approached Michael, and extended his hand.

"Blake McMillan," he stated with a definite air of superiority. "You must be Michael Stafford."

Michael assessed this newcomer with a jaundiced eye. The man knew how to dress, he would give him that. He wore a very expensive navy-blue Armani suit, and a matching tie that probably cost more than any one of Michael's barn staff made in a month. His perfectly pressed dress shirt complemented the suit perfectly. His shoes were also of the highest quality, most likely also Armani. Michael shook Blake's hand firmly, and looked him squarely in the eye. He wasn't going to let this wealthy nabob run roughshod over him on his own property. No, not at all. "Yes, I'm Michael. Welcome to Stafford Oaks Farm, Mr. McMillan."

"Call me Blake, please." The blighter even made that assurance sound condescending. Michael knew he and Blake were not going to be fast friends. He hoped the man's stay would be short. Michael also didn't like the way Blake was looking at Jessica. It was almost as if he were sizing her up for his next meal. Michael's stomach clenched, as a wave of possessive anger rolled over him. There was no way this interloper was getting anywhere near Jessica if Michael had his way, and he vowed he would.

Jessica pushed Hailey in her wheelchair into the manor, and showed her where she would be staying. "This house is awesome, Jess," Hailey exclaimed. "It's just what I imagined an English manor house to look like."

"It is beautiful, and I understand Michael spent a lot of money renovating it," Jessica responded.

"I wasn't kidding about Michael, Jess. He's gorgeous. And that accent . . ." She sighed in rapture.

"About Michael," Jess began, not sure exactly how to tell Hailey about their relationship. She really wasn't quite sure how to describe it. Were they lovers? The term seemed pretty risqué, but the labels boyfriend and girlfriend seemed to trivialize what they had together in her mind.

"What, Jess?" Hailey said. "What about Michael?"

"Well, our relationship has gone beyond a trainer/student relationship. We're actually seeing each other romantically. In fact, don't tell him I said this, but I think I'm falling in love with him."

Hailey squealed in delight. "Jess! That's great! I'm so happy for you. I know I kid you about how good looking he is, but he seems like a really good guy. I'm so glad I'm here now to get to know him better. Maybe he'll be a part of the family soon."

Jess hugged Hailey and couldn't help feeling her heart swell with joy. "I hope so, Hails, I really hope so."

~ ~ ~

While the commotion was going on with the new arrivals at the manor, Lionel was using the round pen to try Monty Roberts' Join-Up training method with Rocky. Over the last few days, the gelding had been accepting more and more physical contact from Lionel without flinching or shying away, and Lionel was extremely encouraged. Lionel felt the time was right to advance his relationship with Rocky, and Join-Up seemed to be the ideal way to do that in a cooperative, non-threatening way.

The purpose of Join-Up, as put forward in Monty Roberts' books and videos and on his website, is for the horse owner/trainer to develop a relationship of mutual concern and respect with the horse using the horse's own natural language.

The process started with the horse being given free movement in a round pen, with the human trainer creating a somewhat fearful environment for the horse, but allowing the horse to run away from the fearful object within established limits of the round pen.

This was the aspect of the training that Lionel was most apprehensive about. Rocky was already fearful of humans in general because of his past abuse, so encouraging that fear through any action on his part was problematic in Lionel's mind.

As it turned out, Lionel's worries were justified. As soon as Rocky realized he was free within the confines of the round pen, any time that Lionel approached him, flicking a rope line, he fled, galloping at full speed around the perimeter of the round pen, eyes wide open, a panicked expression on his face. Lionel was worried that Rocky might hurt himself running as fast and as mindlessly as he was around the perimeter of the pen, but instinct told him not to interfere, but to let Rocky work this out for himself. Gradually, over a period of several minutes, Rocky tired of running, and slowed his pace to a reasonable canter, then to a slower, more controlled trot. Lionel also noticed that Rocky was licking and chewing, and his ears were pricked toward him. Now that Rocky was aware of his presence and exhibiting interest in a curious rather than fearful way, Lionel implemented the second, most critical part of Join-Up, the invitation to the horse to accept him and trust him as a leader.

To do this, Lionel turned away from Rocky, and broke eye contact, thereby inviting him to approach him with trust and submission. Lionel waited for what felt like hours, but had to have been only a few minutes, when he felt Rocky's muzzle nudge his shoulder in a gesture of curiosity and trust, and stood there, without a trace of fear. Lionel, unaware until that very moment that he had been holding his breath, exhaled and was suddenly overcome with a wave of incredibly strong feelings. The first thought that came to mind was that he didn't deserve the complete trust this poor abused horse was giving him. He reflected on his behavior of the past few months, especially toward his best friend Michael, and most recently his very uncharacteristic willingness to jeopardize a horse's life, and was overcome.

Powerful emotions poured forth from Lionel as if a dam had burst, pouring wave after wave of grief, anger, fear, shame, and finally relief over him. The feelings were almost too strong to bear, and he sobbed uncontrollably, still standing in the middle of the round pen, with Rocky patiently standing at his shoulder, curious but not afraid. After several minutes of a deep, purging cry, Lionel looked up toward the heavens. *Nigel, my love, I miss you so much. I've completely lost my way. Please help me find my way back.*

Lionel received no clear answer to his plea, but knew that from this day forward, his life would be irrevocably changed. Using the front of his polo shirt to dry the tears from his face, Lionel turned to Rocky, quietly praised him for his courage and trust, clipped the lead rope back to his halter, and returned him to his stall. There was no way he was going to try any further training today. Avoiding the new arrivals, he went into his bedroom and closed the door. He had a lot of soul searching to do.

Chapter 19

The next morning, Jessica looked out the window of her room, her gaze following Michael and Blake as Michael gave her potential sponsor a tour of the yard, and finally took him into the stables to introduce him to Tempest. Jessica knew she should be accompanying the pair on the tour, but she couldn't make herself endure any more time in close proximity to Blake, especially when Michael was also present. Ever since Blake arrived yesterday, there had been a handful of occasions where she would swear that he had maneuvered a situation so they could be alone, then he would touch her hand, or her arm, or just for a second or two put his hand on her back, while speaking to her about her progress with Tempest, in such a way that she couldn't object, but knew by his heated looks that he was pressing for more. It was very frustrating, and worse, she realized that Michael was noticing Blake's attempts at flirtation and had grown more distant and angry as the day progressed. Jessica didn't know what to do.

The tension between Michael and Blake was palpable, and she didn't have any time alone with Michael to explain that she was trying to be polite to Blake, but was doing everything she could to keep him at arm's length. It was so difficult for Jessica to walk the fine line she needed to in order to maintain Blake's support, but discourage his advances.

To add to Jessica's frustration, Liz and Hailey had noticed Blake's attitude toward Jessica and the heated glances he made no effort to hide. Liz had taken her aside and tried to warn her. "Jess, be careful with Blake. He doesn't seem to understand that just by buying you a horse doesn't mean he's bought you as well."

Jessica groaned her frustration. "How am I supposed to do that, Liz? Blake is a man who is used to having women much more beautiful and sophisticated than me throw themselves at him without shame, and isn't accustomed to rejection. Tell me how to discourage him without jeopardizing my chances to have him as a sponsor, and I'll be eternally grateful."

Liz had shrugged in sympathy, clearly at a loss to help. "It may be that you just have to tell him point blank how things are. If he decides not to support you, so be it. If the USDF knew that he was sexually harassing you to keep his support, they would end their relationship and find another sponsor. I'll make sure of it."

"You make it sound so easy." Jessica sighed. "All right, Liz. That's exactly what I'll do." Jessica had resolved that first thing tomorrow she would do just that, and turned to go up to her room.

As she turned, Liz had reached out to touch Jess's arm to stop her for just a moment. There was something else she was curious about, and needed to ask Jess to make sure she understood. "Jess," Liz said. "What's going on between you and Michael? I sense that he's more to you than just a trainer. Am I right?"

Jessica blushed a bright red and looked anywhere but in Liz's eyes. "Yes, Liz. Michael and I have grown very close during my time here. In fact, I think I'm falling in love with him. Better yet, I think he feels the same, although he hasn't actually said the words yet." As she confessed her feelings, Jessica looked up and met Liz's eyes. Liz could see the love reflected there and smiled broadly.

"That's great, Jess. I'm so happy for you."

"Please don't say anything to Michael. I'm not certain of his feelings, and don't want him to feel any pressure, especially with Blake here right now."

"My lips are sealed." Liz responded with a smile.

Jessica had squeezed Liz's hand and then had gone up to her room.

Jessica and Michael had decided to curtail their nightly encounters while Blake was in the house, and as a result, Jessica had trouble sleeping. She missed the closeness she and Michael had developed in their short time together. She smiled to herself as she reflected how her relationship with Michael had blossomed over the past month. She knew without a doubt that she was falling in love with him. When they were together, there was no one else, and there was no place she'd rather be. When she considered that one of them would win and one would lose in this competition for Tempest, her heart sank. She wished with all her heart there could be a way they could both benefit from this competition, but after racking her brain, she couldn't think of a thing.

Realizing that there was no way she was going to sleep, and feeling a bit hungry, she decided to raid Michael's kitchen. Maybe a cup of tea and a fresh blueberry scone would help her relax so she could get some sleep. She would need her rest to stay sharp tomorrow. It had become clear from Blake's behavior toward her as she showed him to his room that he expected Jessica to be grateful to him for offering to buy her a horse. Jessica was grateful, of course, but she got the definite impression that Blake expected her to show her gratitude by sleeping with him.

Jessica blushed again as she recalled her confession to Liz, but the more she thought about it, she was certain that Michael was her perfect match. She vowed she would get up the courage to confess her true feelings to him as soon as they were alone. Unfortunately, that opportunity would probably have to wait until Blake left to go back to the States. Jessica's stomach growled, and she realized that she really hadn't eaten that much for dinner. Stress caused by Blake's visit and Michael's reaction to Blake and his treatment of her had effectively ruined her appetite. Now, however, she had relaxed a bit, and was ready for some sustenance, even if was only a midnight snack. She made her way down to the kitchen and put some water on to boil. After starting the teakettle, she searched in the cupboard and found tea leaves, then found a scone in the bread box on the counter.

Suddenly, she felt another presence in the room, and looked up to see Blake in the kitchen doorway, watching her intently. A cold chill washed over Jessica when she saw the intensity of Blake's stare. She instantly regretted her decision to venture into the kitchen alone, and looked around desperately for a possible excuse to make her escape. Unfortunately, Blake had already seen the teapot on to boil, and the tea leaves and scone on the counter.

"I see I wasn't the only one with hunger pangs," Blake said, his gaze never leaving Jessica's face. "Do you mind if I join you?"

"No, of course not," Jessica responded, attempting as best she could to exhibit a casual demeanor. "I was just making some tea. There are scones in the bread box if you want one."

"Actually, I see something far sweeter and much more desirable right in front of me," Blake, with a lascivious smile on his face, approached Jessica, and before she realized his intention, gripped her upper arms to hold her in place, and kissed her. Stunned at Blake's blatant aggression, Jessica froze in place, and he pinned her against the kitchen counter. Blake's kiss was anything but gentle. His cool, thin lips pressed harshly to Jessica's mouth, crushing her lips against her teeth. Jessica actually tasted blood from the assault on her mouth. She attempted to struggle, but Blake's superior strength held her in place, and she couldn't move. She knew from the pain in her arms that his violent grip there was causing bruises.

Jessica resisted Blake's attempt to thrust his tongue into her mouth, and frantically tried to think about how she could extract herself from this situation with her dignity and self-respect intact, when she saw Michael appear at the kitchen door. *Thank God! Michael, please help me!* Then, to Jessica's shock, Michael's expression changed from surprise, to hurt, to anger in quick succession, then he spun around and left the room. Jessica's heart sank. *No! He thinks I've betrayed him just like Emma.* Her heart sank, and she must have let some of the tension leave her body, because Blake let go of his grip of her arms, and started moving his hands over her body.

Blake had started to pull Jessica's T-shirt up so he could have easier access to her breasts, and she knew she needed to act quickly or lose control completely. She fought her instinct to panic and in her now adrenaline-fueled sense of awareness realized that Blake's legs were straddling her own leaving her legs relatively free and his most vulnerable spot unguarded. She quickly judged her ability to use her knee to catch Blake in the groin, and launched her defense.

Her knee caught Blake exactly where it needed to and he immediately collapsed, howling in pain, and cursing her as loudly as he could, considering his throat was constricted in pain. Jessica took advantage of his collapse to run from the kitchen, her thoughts entirely on finding Michael. Unfortunately, Blake recovered more quickly than she anticipated, and, with a furious growl, lunged at Jessica. She narrowly escaped his outstretched hands, and realized that if she truly wanted to be safe from Blake, she would have to go back to her bedroom and lock the door.

Jessica hurried back to her room and quickly locked the door. Not long after that, she heard Blake's footsteps prowling the hallway. He stopped outside her door, and tested the knob. When he realized the door was locked, she heard him curse under his breath. Jessica waited, knowing that if he really wanted to, Blake could break through the flimsy lock on Jessica's bedroom door, but Blake, likely knowing any further efforts on his part to get to Jessica would wake the others, stepped away from the door.

Jessica knew this would be her best chance to let Blake know exactly how she felt, just in case her response to him in the kitchen wasn't clear enough. She walked closer to the door to ensure that he heard her loud and clear without alerting the entire house of what had happened. "Mr. McMillan, I hope it's clear to you by now that I have no interest in a relationship with you beyond your sponsorship of me as a dressage rider. If you agree to abide by my rules, I won't report your behavior to the authorities or the USDF and we can continue as sponsor and beneficiary. If you can't, then we must end this relationship here and now."

Blake growled his response. "After what just transpired, Miss Warren, I want nothing further to do with you. Clearly you have no interest in associating with me other than to take my money. Under those circumstances, I choose to spend my money elsewhere. After tonight, you will never see me again. I trust that my actions will convince you not to involve the authorities in this matter. What happened between us was simply a misunderstanding. Nothing more. Good night, and good luck."

Blake continued down the hallway to his room. She heard his door close, and no further sounds came from that direction. She sighed in relief and took a quick inventory of her physical condition. Other than bruised and cracked lips, and bruises circling her upper arms where Blake had gripped her, she was unharmed. She walked to her bed, and sat on the edge, collecting her thoughts. Where had Michael gone after walking away, and what was he thinking? It was clear that he believed she and Blake were locked in a passionate embrace, and that she had betrayed him. Would he believe her when she told him the truth?

More importantly, could she forgive him for thinking the worst of her and leaving her to fight Blake off on her own? She thought about trying to find Michael and talking to him right away, but decided against it. In the state he was in, there was little likelihood he would listen to her explanation. It would have to wait until morning. With a heavy sigh, Jessica laid back on top of the coverlet and stared at the ceiling knowing she wouldn't be getting any sleep tonight.

Hailey closed the door to her bedroom and reflected over what she had just heard. She had gotten up and was maneuvering her wheelchair toward the bathroom, when she heard voices at the top of the stairs and stopped. From what she had heard, she surmised that Blake had tried to sexually assault Jess, and that Jess had rebuffed him enough to make him extremely angry. She grinned to herself. *Good for you, Jess*. Unfortunately, it also sounded as though Jess no longer had a sponsor. Although she knew Jess would be devastated if she couldn't win Tempest, she also knew that Jessica would never allow herself to be some man's plaything in exchange for an expensive horse. Jessica did the only thing she could have done and stayed true to herself, but there would be consequences. There would certainly be a lot to talk about tomorrow. She quietly resumed her trip to the bathroom, returned to her room, and went back to sleep.

Michael stalked out of the house, his fists clenched, his jaw locked. He had the urge to hit something, hard. How dare she? How dare Jessica string him along and lead him to believe she cared for him when all along she was waiting for her rich, powerful lover to arrive and sweep her off her feet? *What I fool I was, falling for her sweet, innocent, wholesome facade. She looked anything but sweet and innocent in Blake McMillan's arms.*

Earlier that night, he had been in his bed missing not only her soft, warm, pliant body in his arms, but also the playful banter they usually shared and quiet acceptance he felt when with her when he heard her leave her room to go down to what he suspected was the kitchen for a late-night snack. He was smug in the realization that she couldn't sleep either, most likely missing him as much as he missed her. He had expected to find her alone and share at the very least a midnight snack, and possibly more, when he approached the kitchen and found Jessica passionately embracing Blake McMillan. In that instant, shock led to hurt, which led quickly to anger. *I'm such a fool.*

He marched angrily out to the stable, hoping to find some solace in the company of the slumbering horses, but even there, his memories of their nights making love in the loft came back to him, angering him even further. Tempest was awake in his stall, and nickered to Michael as he walked down the aisle. Michael knew he couldn't approach the stallion in his present state, or Tempest would sense the tension and respond accordingly. He took some deep, cleansing breaths, forced himself to relax, and felt the tension in his body ebb. Once he felt calm, he walked over and rubbed the stallion's neck absently.

"How could I have been so wrong about her, old man?" he asked the stallion. "She seemed so honest and uncomplicated." Tempest nudged Michael then rested his head against Michael's chest as if offering him comfort. Michael scratched his forehead. "Thanks, boy. I appreciate the sympathy. I'll need more of that in the coming weeks." He left the barn and walked around the property seeking some relief from the tremendous hurt he was feeling as a result of Jessica's betrayal. Unfortunately, everywhere he walked on the property triggered a memory of time spent with Jessica. Eventually, he made his way back to the house, half expecting to find Jessica still in Blake's arms, but to his surprise, the kitchen was deserted. Apparently, the pair had decided to take their reunion to a more private location, either her room or his most likely. He noticed that the teakettle was still heating on the stove and turned the heat off. Surely, neither would be returning tonight. As he went back up to his bedroom to attempt to sleep, Michael resolved that Jessica would feel his displeasure at her betrayal tomorrow.

Jessica awoke the next morning after a fitful night dreading meeting both Blake and Michael, but resolved to straighten things out with both of them. She dragged herself out of bed, and opened her bedroom door as silently as possible, then scanned the hallway to see if anyone else was up. Thankfully, the first person she saw was Liz, who was up and had already showered, anticipating watching a training session with Michael coaching Jessica on Tempest later that morning. Jessica rushed to take a shower herself, then made her way to breakfast. She was feeling a bit sore from her altercation with Blake last night, but she covered the bruises on her arms with a long-sleeved t-shirt and her bruised lips didn't appear too swollen after she applied cold water to them after her shower.

"Good morning," Liz greeted warmly. "Are you ready for our training session today? I've been very impressed with the progress you and Michael have made together, and I really want to see you work Tempest in person."

"Sure," Jessica replied. "As soon as I finish my scone and have some coffee, we can go out."

"Have you seen Michael?" Liz asked. "I thought he'd be coaching you while I watch you this morning."

"I haven't seen him since last night," Jessica replied. "Have you seen Blake?"

"He left a note saying that he was going to London for a few days, and didn't know when he would be back." Liz said. "Business apparently."

"So he's gone?" Jessica couldn't believe her ears. She breathed a sigh of relief. Then, her heart sank. She needed to see Michael as soon as possible and explain to him that what he saw was not as it appeared. Although she knew that her future with Tempest was probably non-existent after what had happened last night, her thoughts were entirely on Michael, and doing everything she could to preserve their relationship. She had to talk to him.

Jessica finished her breakfast, and she and Liz made their way to the barn. Jessica tacked up Tempest, all the while looking toward the house anticipating Michael's appearance at any time. Finally, after she had donned her safety helmet and mounted Tempest, and Liz was talking to her in the outdoor arena, Michael exited the house and approached them. Jessica tensed when she saw Michael's demeanor. He walked rigidly, his fists clenched at his sides as if he were struggling to hold himself back from doing something physically harmful to someone. When he looked at Jessica, she felt his cold, hostile stare, and knew she had her work cut out for her. The only feeling she got from him was anger, even hatred. She shuddered inwardly.

Liz appeared not to notice Michael's hostility, but Jessica had become sensitive to Michael's moods and immediately stiffened. Tempest picked up Jessica's tension, and began swishing his tail nervously in response. Jessica tried to quiet the stallion, but her efforts weren't working, so Liz suggested she start working to alleviate the tension. As they began trotting around the arena, Jessica relaxed, and Tempest responded right away, relaxing and moving forward with his usual confidence.

Michael had to exercise superhuman control to stop himself from expressing his anger and disgust with Jessica in front of Liz. Later, when they were alone, he would make certain that Jessica knew exactly how he felt about her blatant betrayal. As he watched Jessica ride, he seethed at the improvements in her riding that he personally had provided her through his training. He also, however, saw some flaws in her riding that he felt a perverse pleasure in pointing out to her, now being as good a time as any to do so, in his mind.

"Jessica, watch your position," Michael called out. "You're not centered as you should be."

"All right." Jessica re-adjusted her seat and checked her position. Everything seemed in correct alignment from what she could see.

Liz shot a quizzical look at Michael. Jessica's position looked fine. Michael ignored her glance, focusing completely on Jessica and Tempest.

Once Tempest had been sufficiently warmed up, Liz asked Jessica to start riding the Grand Prix Special test, so she could get a feel for where the two needed work. Jessica began to do so, when Michael interjected again.

"I'm not sure she's ready to ride the entire test, Liz. She's been having trouble with the transitions between piaffe and passage, and I think we should be working on that instead."

Jessica heard Michael's comment to Liz, and her temper flared. They had been practicing those transitions frequently, and had gotten them nearly perfect. There was no need to go over them again. She stopped Tempest and walked him over to Liz and Michael to make that exact point. Michael saw that Jessica was irritated with him, and smiled to himself. *Good. It serves her right. It's the least I owe her after what she's done to me.*

Liz didn't understand the dynamic that was playing out between Michael and Jessica, but decided that it wouldn't hurt to work the transitions quickly before moving on to ride the test, so at Liz's request, Jessica ground her teeth and took Tempest to the middle of the arena.

They started with several steps of passage, transitioned to ten steps of piaffe, then transitioned back into the passage. From Jessica's perspective the stallion was working very well, and she was ready to move forward, but Michael wouldn't let them go. The transition from piaffe back to passage was never good enough for him, no matter what she did. She finally asked him as sarcastically as possible what he suggested she do to improve their performance.

"You need to use the spur at exactly the point of the transition, to keep him coming through from behind all the way through it," he said, putting as much exasperation in his voice as he possibly could. His tone was one of condescension and long-suffering frustration. "We've gone over this many times. Use the spur, and if the spur isn't enough, tap him with the whip." Jessica had noted that Tempest was losing patience with this constant repetition, and was tensing and irritated. He was pinning his ears and swishing his tail and had become extremely sensitized to her aids. She knew if they continued in this vein, he would eventually erupt in a nasty temper tantrum. She would be damned, however, if she would let Michael see her apprehension. He would just use it to accuse her of being a timid rider, afraid to assert herself with the willful stallion.

Liz attempted to intervene. "Michael, I don't think . . ."

"Fine," Jessica said, her temper near the boiling point. Tempest, sensing her anger, and not knowing whether or not he was the source, shook his head, and snorted his confusion and irritation. Jessica knew Tempest was warning her that his tolerance was nearing an end, but she was so angry at Michael's attitude toward her, she ignored the signs. It hurt Jessica deeply that Michael had seemingly forgotten all of the time they had spent together, and in one brief, fleeting moment was willing to believe that she was just another untrustworthy woman like Emma without even taking the time to assess the reality of the situation.

Just as Jessica was poised to again execute the transition, one of Michael's barn cats streaked through the arena, chasing a mouse she had seen on the other side, going right between Tempest's back legs. As far as Tempest was concerned, that was the last straw.

The stallion gathered himself and leaped into the air, twisting his body, then upon hitting the ground threw his head down between his front legs and executed a vicious buck, then spun on his hindquarters ninety degrees and bolted. Jessica tried valiantly to hold on, but when Tempest bucked, she lost her balance, and when he spun there was no way she could hold on. She was launched out of the saddle, and landed on her shoulder, then her helmeted head hit the ground hard. Michael and Liz heard the impact. When the dust cleared, Jessica laid still on the ground, not moving at all.

"Oh my God, Jess!" Liz cried, as she ran to Jessica's side.

Michael, his heart in this throat, was right there with her, berating himself as a fool for pushing Jessica and Tempest until the horse finally had enough. *Damn it, you should have known better than to take your temper out in this way. You may have just killed the woman you love.* Yes, even after her betrayal, Michael knew he was still in love with her. As soon as he reached Jessica, he could see that she was unconscious, and unresponsive to Liz's attempts to communicate, but still breathing. He took out his cell phone and called for an ambulance. One of his barn workers heard the commotion and caught Tempest, who was now acting like a tired old plow horse, and took him into the barn to untack and put away.

Jessica had still not regained consciousness when the ambulance arrived, and her shoulder appeared to be twisted in an unnatural position, so Michael surmised that she had either dislocated it or suffered a broken collar bone. The EMT's confirmed the collar bone was indeed broken, and gently placed Jessica on a gurney. As soon as she was placed in the ambulance they rushed her to the hospital in Guildford. Hailey had been in the house eating a leisurely breakfast when she heard the commotion and rushed out as quickly as she could using her prosthetics and crutches to see what had happened to Jessica.

"Michael, what happened?" Hailey cried.

"It's Jess, Hailey. Tempest threw a temper tantrum and bucked her off. The paramedics think she has a concussion and a broken collar bone. We're taking her to the hospital now."

"I want to go too." Hailey looked at Michael, then Liz. "How could this happen? Jess and Tempest had been getting along fine. You even said that they are a brilliant pair. What changed?"

Liz couldn't help but wonder the same thing. According to Jessica, she and Michael cared deeply for each other, and their training sessions with Tempest had been going well. How had things changed in just the past twenty-four hours?

"Yes, Michael," Liz said. "I've been watching you and Jess work with Tempest for weeks now. There has never been any problem like this. Can you explain what's going on?"

Michael grimaced as if in pain. "It was all my fault. I was angry with Jessica and provoked her into losing her temper. While we were arguing, neither of us realized the Tempest was becoming more and more agitated. All it took was the cat to provide the trigger, and he went off. I'm so sorry. I want you to know that I love Jessica very much, and whatever happens between her and Blake McMillan, my feelings won't change. I'll do everything I can to support your sister with Tempest."

Liz and Hailey both stared at Michael in shock. They looked at each other, then back at Michael to make sure he was serious. Finally, Hailey spoke. "Oh, Michael, didn't Jess tell you? Blake tried to force himself on her last night and she fought back. He got angry and made it very clear that he was no longer interested in sponsoring her. He left early this morning. Good riddance if you ask me."

Michael was stunned at Hailey's revelation. The next wave of emotion that crashed over him was pure rage, first at Blake then at himself. Apparently, the scene he had walked in on wasn't a passionate embrace but a sexual assault, and he had walked away and left Jessica to fend for herself. He was not only an idiot, he was nearly as much of a bastard as Blake himself. If Jessica ever spoke to him again, he had a lot of groveling and explaining to do. He vowed then and there that whatever he had to do to make Jessica his forever, he would do it. This was the woman he loved and whom he wanted to spend the rest of his life with. Of this, he had no doubts.

The three of them rushed to Michael's car and followed the ambulance to the hospital. Hailey and Liz took care of the admission paperwork in the Emergency Room, as the doctors and nurses examined Jessica. While Jessica was still unconscious, they set her collarbone, and wrapped the shoulder so she couldn't displace the bone if she regained consciousness and was disoriented. As they were finishing the wrapping, Jessica moaned as the pain penetrated her consciousness and she slowly began to awaken. The medical team in the ER gave her morphine for the pain, and Jessica soon calmed. Hailey and Liz accompanied Jessica into the treatment area, but Michael decided that he might not be welcome, so he paced in the waiting room and hoped that Liz and Hailey would keep him informed of Jessica's condition.

While he paced, Michael continued to berate himself for his behavior with Jessica. It was entirely his fault that Jessica was hurt, possible permanently injured. He couldn't deny that it was their argument that had caused Tempest to be so on edge that all it took was a crazy cat to set him off. He would not be able to live with himself if Jessica suffered permanent injury due to his childish temper tantrum. After nearly an hour of anxious waiting, Hailey emerged from the treatment area and informed Michael that Jessica was awake, and other than suffering from a throbbing headache and the pain from her broken collarbone, she seemed to be all right. The doctors had diagnosed a severe concussion, however, and were requiring Jessica spend at least twenty-four hours in the hospital for observation.

"Can I see her?" Michael asked.

"Actually, she was asking for you," Hailey said. "Just don't stay too long. She needs her rest."

"No problem." Michael followed Hailey back to Jessica's room, where he found Liz sitting by the bed, holding Jessica's hand and trying to make sure she was comfortable. Jessica looked pale, and weak, but he could tell that she was aware of her surroundings, and didn't appear to have suffered any brain damage from her fall. Thank God she had been wearing a helmet. If she hadn't, she would probably be dead.

Michael shuddered with the realization of how close he had come to losing her. He vowed this would never happen again. Not while she was in his life. If he had his way, that would be from now on. Forever.

"Liz, honestly, they have me on so much pain medication, I'm not sure I can stand even if I wanted to," Jessica was trying to reassure Liz that she wasn't going to try to walk out of the hospital before the doctors gave her permission to leave.

Jessica looked up when Michael appeared at the door. She could feel the tension he was holding. She smiled in an attempt to put him at ease and to reassure him that she was going to be all right, and that she wasn't blaming him for her fall. "Michael, hi. Please come in." She cast a speaking look at Liz, "Liz was just leaving, and taking Hailey with her." Liz nodded and drew Hailey out of the room, leaving Jessica and Michael alone.

"Jess, I don't know what to say," Michael started, guilt edging his voice. "This is all my fault. I should never have argued with you while you were riding Tempest. My actions were unforgivable."

Jessica looked at Michael, her gaze unwavering. "I have to take some of the blame as well, Michael," Jessica responded. "I let my temper get the best of me, too. I couldn't let your criticisms go without doing everything I could to prove you wrong. I could tell Tempest was getting tense, but quite frankly I didn't care. I only wanted to prove you wrong."

She plucked absently at the blanket on her hospital bed as she considered what to say next. "About Blake, I know how it must have looked to you to see Blake with me in the kitchen. If I had actually been making out with him as it probably looked like I was, if I were you, I would have been mad, too. I want to make sure you know it wasn't what you thought. That being said, I am hurt and disappointed that you were so quick to draw the worst conclusion about me and didn't allow yourself to believe I was different from Emma."

Michael forced himself to look into Jessica's eyes. "Hailey told me what really happened last night with Blake. I owe you an apology for assuming the worst about you. I should have known you better than to assume that you and Blake were lovers behind my back."

Jessica frowned. "Hailey knew? She must have overheard my ultimatum to Blake after I escaped from him and locked myself into my room. What actually happened last night was that Blake found me in the kitchen making tea, and forced himself on me. He pinned me to the counter, and gripped my arms so that I couldn't defend myself, or push him away." She showed him the bruises circling her upper arms as proof of Blake's brutality. "It was only the fact that he left my legs relatively free, and I was able to knee him forcefully in the groin that I was able to escape him and lock myself in my bedroom for the rest of the night."

"I'm so sorry, Jess. The fact that I left you to fend for yourself against a brutal predator shames me irrevocably. I wonder why you're still speaking to me at all." If Michael felt guilty before, he felt even more so now. It had been so easy for him to put Jessica in the same class as Emma without even a thought for how different the two of them were, and how much more he cared for Jessica than he ever had for Emma. Coupled with his own guilt was a tremendous anger at Blake for his behavior. He felt like tearing the bloke's head off. No man should ever treat a woman the way Blake had treated Jessica. The fact that he had brutally attacked her and might even have raped her drove him insane with anger. He wanted to find the man and rip him apart with his bare hands.

At that moment, the doctor treating Jessica entered the room, and asked Michael to leave so he could examine Jessica and update her on her treatment and status. Michael nodded and went to look for Liz and Hailey. He found them in the waiting area. Hailey confirmed that she had filled Liz in on Blake's behavior with Jessica the night before. Not certain how the two women Jessica loved most in the world would treat him after the way he had behaved, he approached them with a certain amount of caution. "I suppose you both know how much of an ass I've been in the past twenty-four hours." When neither of the women responded immediately, he continued, "I want you both to know that I'm prepared to do anything it takes to convince Jessica that I love her, and that I was completely unjustified in thinking that she was unfaithful to me and that I won't give up until she forgives me and accepts me."

Hailey stood up and walked over to Michael. Her solemn countenance broke into a huge grin, and she threw her arms around Michael and hugged him close. "I can't guarantee anything, Michael, but if you say those words to her, Jess would be crazy to reject you." Liz was also smiling and nodding at him, and Michael breathed a sigh of relief. With these two on his side, he knew the odds of getting Jessica back were in his favor. In the meantime, he was determined that Jess would be well cared for. He had decided that to ensure Jessica wouldn't be alone while she was in the hospital he would be staying with Jessica for the rest of the day, then overnight tonight. Liz and Hailey agreed, and Liz offered to bring Hailey to relieve Michael first thing tomorrow morning.

Michael also realized that Tempest would be missing his regular work unless Liz was able to cover, so he asked her if she could do that. Liz agreed. After bidding Michael a good night, Liz and Hailey left for the farm.

While Michael was out speaking with Hailey and Liz, one of the ER doctors came into Jessica's room to check on her. Jessica looked expectantly at the doctor as he looked at the computer screen next to her bed, and checked her current status. "It appears that at least for the next 24 hours, you'll be our guest, but you'll be happy to know that your collar bone break was clean, and should heal nicely with no complications." After confirming that Jessica's head still ached in the aftermath of her concussion, he assured her that was normal, and that her pain medication should help with that. He did some further tests to determine the extent of any brain trauma cause by the concussion. "By the way, I want to assure you that the fall didn't harm the baby, and we made sure that the pain medication you're taking is safe."

Jessica's heart skipped a beat. "The what?" she asked breathlessly.

"Ah, you didn't know you were pregnant," he said. "That's quite normal. The fetus is only about two to three weeks old, so I'm not surprised you weren't yet aware of it. It's not a problem, is it?"

'No, it's not a problem." Jessica responded, still not quite sure she believed what the doctor was telling her. "Doctor, I would very much appreciate it if you didn't tell anyone about the pregnancy."

"Of course not," the doctor replied. "Doctor-patient confidentiality prohibits me from disclosing your medical condition to anyone that you haven't authorized to have that information."

"Thank you," Jessica said, her mind spinning with this new development. Her head was already hurting, and she was confused and disoriented. She didn't know how she was going to cope with this additional complication, much less think clearly in her current state. She definitely needed to sleep and start the healing process, but she couldn't stop thinking about what the doctor had just revealed. How was she going to tell Michael, and what would his reaction be? Would he be happy, or would he be disappointed? More importantly, since Michael's behavior toward her last evening, how did she feel about their relationship? Jessica had been honest with Michael when she told him how disappointed she was that he so easily believed she was capable of betraying him – that she could not be trusted. Had she been mistaken about his feelings for her? Did he truly love her? Knowing she wouldn't have any of those questions answered tonight, Jessica closed her eyes and eventually drifted into an exhausted sleep.

Michael entered Jessica's darkened room and noticed right away that she had fallen asleep. His gaze searched her face for any signs of pain or discomfort, but she appeared to be sleeping peacefully. He marveled at how beautiful she looked, even after such a traumatic experience. The worry lines on her face had disappeared, and she looked less careworn and much younger, much more innocent. Michael snorted in disgust at himself. *Idiot, she is innocent, it was you that made her out to be less than what she was.* This time he was the accuser, the one who had felt betrayed. He didn't deny how powerful the emotion was once he experienced it for himself. He could now, at least in part, understand why he didn't see that Jessica was in distress that night.

A memory flashed vividly to mind. He had just returned from a trip to France to teach a weekend long clinic near Normandy, and was looking forward to time alone with Emma. To his dismay, Emma angrily confronted him as soon as he walked in the door. "I'm glad you had such a good time in France without me," she said. "It seems that one of the clinic participants posted on your Facebook page about how great a rider you are, and how wonderful it was to ride with you. How could you do this to me?"

"Do what?" he asked. "The woman is simply saying she enjoyed the clinic and wanted to let me know. There's nothing sexual about that." To his mind, it was a totally innocuous comment, but Emma had interpreted it to mean that the woman had slept with him. A much as he insisted the comments were innocent and that he hadn't slept with the woman, Emma refused to believe him. He finally realized how damaging Emma's behavior had been to his psyche, how deeply the hurt had buried itself inside him. Jessica was everything Emma wasn't, yet in a heartbeat he had been willing to believe she had betrayed him. How could he ever make it up to Jessica? Would she ever trust him again? Thank God she had the courage and fortitude to defend herself, or who knows what might have happened.

Upon reflection, he realized that a part of his mistrust of women after Emma was that he never really did learn what had come between them. As best he could remember, after the Olympics, everything had been great. Emma was right there with him when he found and purchased the refurbished manor house in Surrey with land sufficient for building his training yard. Even after Romeo was taken from him, she supported him, although now that he thought about it, he had always had a sneaking suspicion that she was withholding a part of herself from him, almost expecting him to hurt her in some way.

He realized for the first time that there was never a point in their relationship when he felt as though she trusted him completely. As a result, he never felt that they had a soul-deep connection. Not like he had felt with Jessica from the very start. Even then, though, it wasn't until the very last months of their engagement that Emma had started accusing him of cheating on her, and she had been so positive about it. That was the most confusing part of all. He didn't cheat, so there couldn't have been any proof. Something was missing. He just didn't know what.

He remembered that it was soon after he reconnected with Lionel that Emma began to act differently around him. She questioned his relationships with his students, and accused him of spending too much time away from her when he taught at clinics around the UK and Europe. When he traveled to teach lessons to female students, she accused him of having affairs with them, to the point that he actually considered doing it, since it appeared that she expected it of him. In truth, he could have, because with his Olympic success and his good looks and approachable demeanor, women flirted with him and offered themselves to him all the time. Nevertheless, he'd remained faithful to her. He'd never cheated. When she finally left him, citing his unfaithfulness as the reason, he was beside himself with frustration and anger. The fact that she'd found someone else within weeks after breaking off their engagement didn't help. Maybe she was the one who was cheating, he thought. It certainly seemed that way. All he knew was that he was devastated, his ability to trust seriously damaged.

Jessica stirred, mumbled a bit, and tried to shift position. She grimaced in pain as her movement jostled her broken collarbone, but she didn't wake. She re-settled, finding a more comfortable position, and quieted. Michael settled as best he could in the vinyl padded chair next to her bed, and kept watch as she slept.

Jessica woke up the next morning feeling as if she had been hit by a truck. Her body ached all over, and her head throbbed. She blinked at the bright light streaming in her hospital room window and looked to her right to find Michael, his long legs stretched out in front of him and crossed at the ankles, his arms crossed, and his head slumped down to his chest, sleeping. Her heart warmed to see him there, obviously having spent the night in a most uncomfortable position, just to make sure she wasn't alone. She took a few moments as he slept to study him and to reflect what had happened over the past 24 hours.

Obviously, Michael had jumped to a mistaken conclusion about Jessica's character and in doing so, had hurt her badly. Even clearer to her was the fact that he very much regretted his actions, and believed her account of Blake's assault on her. If she wasn't mistaken, Michael would continue to blame himself for her fall, and that guilt would drive his behavior toward her unless she could find a way to convince him that if she could find it in her heart to forgive him, he should also forgive himself.

More importantly, how was she going to tell him about the baby? Her hand moved instinctively to her abdomen in a gesture of protection. Would he be happy, or would he urge her to end the pregnancy? Would he offer to marry her purely out of a sense of obligation, or did he love her as much as she knew she loved him? The questions whirled around Jessica's already aching head, and no answers would come.

As those thoughts whirled through her mind, Michael stirred, then slowly woke up. He stretched, and worked the kinks out of his shoulders and neck, and stretched his arms and legs. He reminded Jessica of a panther she had seen at the zoo, all lithe grace and leashed power. He noticed her perusal, and smiled, leaned toward her and reached for her hand.

"Good morning. How are you feeling?" he asked. "Did you sleep well?"

"As well as can be expected, I guess," she responded. "How about you? Did you sleep well? It couldn't have been comfortable sleeping in that chair all night."

"I'm fine." Michael hesitated. There was so much yet to be said between them, but he sensed that this wasn't the right time to discuss serious personal matters. She was still in a great deal of pain, and he wasn't yet sure exactly how to move forward knowing he was responsible for her being here in the hospital to begin with. At that moment, a nurse entered the room to examine Jessica, and was soon followed by a hospital volunteer with breakfast.

"I'll go and get something to eat, and be back in a few minutes," he told her. "Liz should be here soon with Hailey to take my place." He reached for Jessica's hand, pressed a kiss on the back of it, winked at her and left the room. He walked down the hall to the elevators and proceeded to the ground floor hospital cafeteria. He ate breakfast quickly, then walked back toward the elevators.

He heard his name being called, and saw Liz and Hailey entering the hospital. He waited for them to join him, and together they proceeded to Jessica's room. As they walked, he filled them in on Jessica's condition.

"Look who I found," Michael announced as they entered the room.

"Hey guys. It's good to see you." Jessica tried to put on the best possible face, but she could tell her sister and friend were still very concerned for her.

"Liz and I decided that I would stay with you this morning, then Liz will come this afternoon and keep you company," Hailey explained.

Jessica was frustrated that they believed she needed to be watched every minute, but she knew better than to argue. "That will be fine. In fact, while you're here Hails, you can fill me in your progress in physical therapy. Maybe we can even find someone here in the hospital that knows a therapist that specializes in treating amputees so you can continue your therapy here in the UK."

Hailey rolled her eyes, but didn't say anything. She knew that Jessica was adamant that she continue to pursue therapy to learn how to use her legs and to strengthen the rest of her body to make optimum use of more modern prosthetics once they had the funds to purchase them. She appreciated Jessica's concern, but felt that, deep down, Jessica was going above and beyond what any reasonable person would expect in her care because she felt somehow responsible for her injuries, and was doing everything in her power to make up for whatever it was she thought she had done. Hailey had tried many times to assure Jessica that the accident wasn't her fault, but Jessica stubbornly refused to acknowledge her. She resolved to talk to Michael about it when they had some time alone. Maybe he could talk some sense into Jessica.

Chapter 20

As Michael drove Liz back to the farm, he felt as though he needed to make sure she knew the entire story of what had happened the night before Jess's fall. "Liz, did Jess tell you how Blake behaved the night before last?"

"No, Michael, she didn't, but Hailey did. I will be calling the USDF immediately and informing them not to accept Blake McMillan as a sponsor for any U.S. rider. Does Jess intend to press charges?"

"My understanding is that in exchange for Blake leaving her alone, she agreed not to press charges. I'm willing to go along with that, if you agree."

"I do. I think we're well rid of Mr. McMillan and hope to never see him again."

"Now," Michael said, changing tack. "About Tempest. Since Jess will be out of commission for a while, I propose that you ride Tempest in her stead to make sure he stays in good shape."

"What about you, Michael?" Liz replied. "Aren't you still going to be riding?"

"Not for the next few days, at least," Michael responded. "I want to take care of Jess while she's recuperating, at least for the first week or two, to make sure she has everything she needs and doesn't re-injure herself trying to do too much too soon."

Liz laughed. "For someone who has known Jess only a few weeks, you certainly know her well. That's exactly what she will try to do, so I advise a great deal of patience in the next two weeks."

Michael smiled back. "Thanks, Liz. I think I'll need it." What Michael didn't tell Liz was that he had been doing some serious thinking over the past few hours and had decided to notify Mendelssohn that he was quitting the competition for Tempest. It was Jessica who deserved him, and he would bow out so that she could have him and fulfill her dreams. He would find some other way to pay for Ian's defense. Maybe the U.S. Dressage Team or the British Dressage Team needed a trainer. He was certain Liz and Jessica would provide him with good recommendations. He just wanted to make Jess happy, and he knew that having Tempest would do just that.

When they reached the farm, Michael encouraged Liz to ride Tempest every day to ensure he stayed in good condition, and that he would be ready for Jessica when she recovered. She agreed that would be best, and went up to her room to change, then proceeded to the barn.

Jessica was released from the hospital the following day, and accepted that her three guardian angels would pamper and coddle her for the next few weeks. After less than a week under Michael, Hailey, and Liz's loving care, Jessica was able to move around the farm with no need of assistance. Liz continued to ride Tempest every day, and Jessica noted that Liz seemed happier and more lighthearted than she had ever seen her. Jessica was troubled, however, by the fact that Michael had stopped riding Tempest. In fact, he didn't even spend any time with the stallion since her injury. She finally got up the courage to ask Michael about it.

Michael led Jessica into the front parlor, escorted her to a comfortable, overstuffed love seat, and sat next to her. He took her hand, and looked into her eyes. He lost himself in their green-gold brightness and swallowed the lump in his throat. "Jess, I've decided to take myself out of the competition for Tempest, and let you have him for yourself." She opened her mouth to respond, but before she could speak, he continued, "When I saw you lying motionless on the ground after your fall, I realized how close I came to losing you, and knew without a doubt that I love you, and that I hated myself for endangering that love with my selfish and immature behavior. I knew that I could never love anyone as much as I love you. I can't foresee a future without you in it, and I can't possibly take advantage of an injury I caused to take your dream away from you."

Jessica's throat constricted, and her eyes glistened. Tears began streaming down her face. She knew in her heart that Michael was serious, that he truly wished only the best for her, and that he was willing to sacrifice his own interests to ensure her happiness. He loved her. If only she could accept his love, but she couldn't. Not until he knew the truth about her, the truth that, once he knew, she was certain would destroy his love. It was time. She had to tell him. Her heart ached knowing the joy of having this deeply sensitive and caring man love her even if it was only for a very short time.

Michael had cupped her face in his hands, and was gently using his thumbs to brush away her tears. He wondered at the sadness he saw in Jessica's eyes. Maybe he had misjudged and she didn't return his feelings. Could it be possible that she didn't love him? He had expected her to be happy, and to return his feelings joyfully. Now, he anxiously waited for her to explain what was causing her unusual reaction to his declaration.

Jessica calmly composed herself and released Michael's hands. "Michael, before we make any decisions about our future, there's something I have to tell you. Once I have, you may want to change your mind about spending the rest of your life with me." She nervously brushed her hands over her thighs, and then clasped them in her lap. Michael reached out and placed a hand over hers. Jessica smiled weakly at him, and began. "When I was young, my family was very close. My mother, father, Hailey and I lived a very ordinary middle-class life in Central Ohio, and were content.

At least Hailey, Mom, and I were content. My father felt some pressure to elevate our financial status, so he left a relatively low paying job that he loved and applied for and got a job with a major corporation in our area. The pay was much better, and he did very well at first, but his superiors expected more and more from him, until he found it difficult to cope with the stress without resorting to alcohol.

"Over time, the alcohol became his answer to any problem he encountered, and our family began to suffer because of it. My parents began to fight over Dad's drinking, and Hailey and I were afraid to be around him. After I graduated high school and went out on my own, working for Liz, I was able to escape for the most part, but I would still have to accompany the family to the annual family reunion picnic a few hours away in Toledo. It never failed that at those picnics, my Dad would drink too much, get angry and belligerent with our relatives, and we would leave in embarrassment. The last year, I decided I wouldn't go and be humiliated by my Dad's behavior ever again. My mother begged me to change my mind and go, in part because between Mom and me we were always able to convince my Dad not to try to drive home, but to let one of us drive instead. Even knowing that, out of pure selfishness, I refused. I reassured my Mom that she would be able to get Dad to turn the car keys over to her, and she would be able to drive them home.

"Evidently, that last year, five years ago, that didn't happen, and my Dad drove drunk, crashed the car, and killed himself and my Mom and permanently injured Hailey." She looked at Michael as tears streamed down her face. His expression was solemn, but otherwise unreadable. "Michael, it was all my fault. I killed my parents and I'm responsible for Hailey's injuries. If I had been there, they would be alive and whole right now. So you see, I'm not worthy of your love. I don't deserve the kind of happiness you're offering me." She stood and turned away from him, unable to see his reaction to her confession. "I understand if you don't ever want to see me again."

During Jessica's recitation, Michael had not once taken his hand from hers, nor had he stopped gazing at her downcast face. Now, as she unselfishly offered to remove herself from his life in the very mistaken belief that he would be disgusted with her for her very normal behavior, he found that he loved her even more, if that was possible. He stood and walked to where she was standing, took her by the shoulders and turned her around to face him. He took her hands, squeezed them, and drew them to his mouth, kissing them both before he spoke. "Sweetheart, what you've told me changes nothing. If anything, I love you even more for your courage and compassion in taking on the responsibility of raising Hailey and caring for her after everything you both have been through.

"What happened to your parents and Hailey was not your fault. There is no way you can be certain that your presence at the picnic would have changed the outcome. Your mother was accustomed to your father's propensities and could have done things to prevent the accident even before they got in that car, but she didn't. Please rest assured that I don't think badly of you for what happened, and I want you to work on forgiving yourself. I'm sure Hailey has forgiven you, if she ever even believed you at fault to begin with."

Jessica looked at Michael and couldn't conceal her shock at what she heard. She searched his eyes for any sign of prevarication, and saw only truth. He still loved her, even knowing what really happened to cause the accident. He was right about Hailey, that she had always assured Jessica she didn't blame her for the accident, but Jessica had rationalized her forgiveness by thinking that she may not have understood the whole story, so Jessica didn't believe herself truly forgiven. Somehow, though, she knew deep down that Hailey understood more than she let on, and that she believed there would not have been anything Jessica could have done to prevent the accident, even if she were there with them.

She smiled brilliantly at Michael, her heart free and unburdened for the first time in years. They stood together and embraced. It felt so good to be held in his strong, protective arms. She knew she would never be able to leave this dear, sweet, and very sexy man.

Michael, for his part, felt lighter than air, his heart free of the mistrust and insecurity that he had been living with since his broken engagement. He stepped out of their embrace and looked down at Jessica. "Now, love, what do you say about taking on Tempest? I was serious when I said I intend to take myself out of the competition and let you ride him. He's yours if you want him. I think you'll do great with him, and I'm willing to tell Mendelssohn that if he balks at the idea."

Jessica refused to meet Michael's gaze, and started to fidget and wring her hands.

"What's wrong, sweetheart? Don't you want to compete with Tempest?"

"I do, Michael, but there's something you should know." Jessica reached for Michael's hands and looked into his eyes. "When I was admitted to the hospital after my fall, they ran a series of blood tests, and discovered that I'm pregnant. You're going to be a father." She looked hesitantly at Michael to gauge his reaction. She wouldn't blame him if he were angry with her for withholding the information and waiting until now to tell him, but knowing everything, maybe he would be willing to overlook the delay.

Michael's face paled for a few seconds, then he cleared his throat, trying to overcome the lump that had suddenly appeared there. A child; conceived in love, a hope for a shared future and a family with the woman he loved. How could he not be thrilled at the thought? His mouth cracked into a huge grin, and he hugged Jessica, picking her up off the floor, and carefully so as not to disturb her broken collar bone, spun her in a circle. By the time they were finished, both were laughing. "This is fantastic!" he cried. "I couldn't be happier." He set Jessica gently back down and flashed her a stern look. "I hope that means that you'll be marrying me sooner rather than later. Maybe even in a few days. As soon as I can get a license."

Jessica was crying with him, and agreed that they should marry in all haste. Then a worried look crossed Jessica's face, and Michael was immediately reaching for her hand. "What's wrong, love? I hope you're not having second thoughts.

"No, it's not that at all," Jessica replied. "It's just that with the pregnancy I won't be able to train Tempest or compete with him in the months leading up to the World Cup. You should be his rider, Michael. You know you have a rapport with him that I never had."

"No, love. I'm not going to spend the entirety of your pregnancy gallivanting all over the world spending all my time riding when I want only to be with you. I'll be distracted, and won't ride my best. Tempest deserves better." He thought for a second. "You know, Liz has been doing great things with Tempest since your injury. Maybe we can convince Mendelssohn that we both agree she should be his rider going forward, at least during the next year leading up to the World Cup."

Michael further explained to Jessica that during the days that Liz had taken over riding Tempest after Jessica's fall, he had noticed that Liz and Tempest had arrived at an understanding, and that the two of them performed admirably together. Occasionally, Michael would, at Liz's request, offer some advice since Liz had little experience riding stallions. Liz had grown to trust Michael's inputs, and with his help, forged a good working partnership with Tempest. For his part, the stallion had grown to respect Liz, and behaved admirably, eventually showing her the same brilliance under saddle that he had shown Michael.

It didn't take long for Jessica to come to the same conclusion that Michael had. Liz would be the perfect partner for Tempest going forward. Now, to convince Liz, then Mendelssohn they were right. As it happened, it wasn't difficult at all to convince Liz that she and Tempest would be great competition partners. The only complicating factor was Liz's husband, who might have balked at maintaining shared custody of their daughter Amy with Liz's demanding competition schedule. However, Liz determined that if she could have Tempest at home in Ohio, and compete for most of the year in the U.S., then a few competition dates in Europe wouldn't be a problem. When consulted, Amy agreed, insisting that everything would be fine, and that between her parents and her aunt Cynthia, all would be well.

The icing on the cake had been when Amy had reminded Rick that in Ohio, children have the right to choose which parent they wish to have custody of them, and the older the child is when they make that choice, the more weight the court gives to their preference. At the age of twelve, Amy was old enough to make that decision for herself without much court interference. Rick ultimately had to agree.

Herr Mendelssohn was surprisingly open to the idea, and since Blake McMillan was no longer willing to purchase Tempest, Mendelssohn and the USET agreed that his sponsorship of Liz as Tempest's rider was the best solution under the circumstances. Both Mendelssohn and Liz agreed that Michael should stay with them as their trainer, and he agreed, subject to Jessica's needs as her pregnancy advanced.

Unfortunately, Jessica and Michael were not able to marry quite as quickly as they had hoped, due to British customs and immigration laws. However, since Jessica had already obtained a visitor visa for the two months she planned to stay in the UK, through some strings thankfully pulled by the US Equestrian Team, Michael was able to obtain a marriage license relatively quickly. Still, the law in the UK required a twenty-eight day wait from the date the license was issued until they could marry.

On the first day they could legally do it, Jessica and Michael were married. Liz, Hailey, Ian, and Lionel were present to celebrate with them, as were Michael's parents.

The couple held a quiet wedding reception for a few friends and family at the manor later that day. After initial toasts and ribald comments were made, and the cake was cut, Lionel drew Michael aside for a private conversation. "First, congratulations, man. Jessica is a fantastic woman; beautiful inside and out. You're a lucky man."

"Thanks Lionel. I agree with you one hundred percent. You've been a great friend to me over the years, Lionel. I really appreciate it."

Lionel began fidgeting, and looked everywhere but at Michael. "That's what I need to talk to you about, Mike. I have a confession to make," Lionel began. "I've not been the friend you thought I was. In fact, I've done several things over the past few months deliberately intended to make your life miserable."

Michael at first thought Lionel was joking, but when he saw Lionel's serious, even shameful expression, he took note. "Tell me, Lionel. What have you done?"

"I'm the person responsible for Emma breaking your engagement," Lionel confessed. "I led her to believe, through the planting of forged love notes and false receipts, that you were having affairs with many of your female clients. I also was the person who tampered with Tempest's stall and left the grain room door open."

"You what?!" Michael's raised voice gained the attention of others standing nearby, so he modulated his tone so others wouldn't overhear. "That can't be true, Lionel. You're my friend, have been since we were kids."

"Unfortunately, it's true. After you turned me in for cheating at the Olympic trials, I hated you. I blamed you for my disgrace and the misfortune that followed me after that, and even for Nigel's death. I vowed to have my revenge by making your life as miserable as you made mine. The rub was, and I didn't realize it until I started working with Rocky, that I and only I was responsible for my lapse in judgment at the trials. I was the one who let my deeply held feelings of insecurity and inadequacy lead me to think that the only way I could win a spot on the team was to cheat."

"The irony," Michael added, "was that you were, and still are, a talented rider in your own right, and probably would have made the team if you hadn't resorted to cheating."

"We'll never know for sure, but you're probably right. In any event, I wanted to tell you how sorry I am that I caused you so much pain. I deeply regret my actions. If there's anything I can do to make it up to you, I am happy to do it."

Michael looked up from their conversation and searched the room for Jessica. His eyes were unerringly drawn to her tall, lithe figure across the room, speaking with his brother Ian. She immediately sensed his gaze, and interrupted her conversation to return it and flashed him a joyful smile. Michael winked at her and grinned, even now feeling the electricity flow between them, then returned his attention to Lionel. "Li, if you hadn't interfered and caused Emma to leave me, I never would have met Jessica, whose presence in my life has made me the happiest of men, so I can't bear a grudge. You did me a tremendous favor in that regard. For that I can only be grateful. However, if you still want to do something that will make me happy, continue your work with an emphasis on abused and neglected horses. You have a gift for it, and can truly make a difference."

Lionel nodded in agreement, grateful that Michael was so forgiving. It would be no hardship for him to focus his business on rehabilitating abused and neglected horses and finding new homes for them. In fact, he looked forward to the challenge. A new life awaited him, and he was eager to step into it.

Time was growing late, and Michael was impatient to spend his wedding night with his new wife. Over the course of the reception, he and Jessica had exchanged heated glances several times, so he knew she felt the same. Finally, the night was drawing near, and their guests were taking their leave. As a courtesy to the fact that this was to be Michael and Jessica's wedding night, Liz and Hailey had offered to spend the night in an Inn in Guildford, so the couple could have the manor house to themselves for the night. They had gratefully accepted the offer. As they sent Hailey and Liz off for the evening, Michael wrapped his arm around Jessica's waist, and started up to what was once his, but was now *their* bedroom. Jessica halted their progress, however, and flashed a worried look at Michael. He frowned in response.

"What's the matter, love?" he asked. "Why are you troubled?"

"Shouldn't we check on the horses, especially Tempest, before we go to bed?"

"I'm sure Tiffany covered night check, but if you insist, we can go out to the barn and make sure the horses are all right." Although impatient to get Jessica alone in his bed, Michael guessed that there was more to Jessica's request than just making sure the horses were settled for the night.

She smiled warmly at him in thanks, and they turned from the stairs to make their way to the barn. Michael removed his arm from Jessica's waist, and grasped her hand, intertwining their fingers as they progressed out the door and out to the peacefully quiet stable.

Once in the stable, Jessica went directly to Tempest's stall. The stallion's head was hanging out over the stall door as if he had been waiting for them to come. He saw the couple and nickered softly to them. Jessica approached him first, and reached up to stroke his forehead. "Somehow I knew you would be waiting for us," Jessica murmured to the stallion fondly. "You think yourself a matchmaker, don't you?" To Michael's surprise, the stallion nodded his head emphatically, then gently rested his forehead against Jessica's chest, sighing with contentment. She laughed and stoked his cheeks, and throatlatch. "You do, you scoundrel. Well, in a way, I think you're right." She looked mischievously at Michael.

Michael heaved an exaggeratedly heavy sigh and rolled his eyes, although Jessica could see the mischievous glint shining from them. "Yes, I suppose he is ultimately responsible. If he had not been available from the beginning, we most likely would never have met, and his misbehavior at critical times, did lead us toward each other." He stroked the stallion's neck fondly, and the horse sighed in response. Michael continued speaking to the stallion, but his patience was nearing an end, "Now that we've gotten that established, I know you'll understand if I take my wife home and consummate this marriage as soon as possible." The stallion nodded again in apparent approval, and the couple left, walking arm in arm, back to their home and the rest of their lives together.

Epilogue

One Year Later

This year's FEI Dressage World Cup Finals were held again in Las Vegas, Nevada, in the MGM Grand Garden Arena, located in the MGM Grand Hotel on the Las Vegas strip. The United States was represented most prominently by Ms. Elizabeth Randall, riding the spectacular Hanoverian stallion, Tempest. The pair were favored to place in the top three, but were expected to have significant competition from riders representing Great Britain and Germany. The competition was fierce, but Liz and Tempest showed their mettle and performed spectacularly, executing flawless tests and amazing the crowd with their brilliance, ultimately winning the championship.

Jessica Warren Stafford and her husband, Michael Stafford, familiar faces to the international competitors and acknowledged training partners with the USDF in support of Elizabeth Randall and Tempest, strode through the aisles of stalls housing the most talented and expensive dressage horses in the world and their riders, grooms and trainers, looking for Liz. Michael carried their three-month-old son, Trevor, in a sling cradled against his chest. The baby, who had his father's black hair and clear blue eyes, was fast asleep cradled comfortably in his father's arms.

"There she is!" Jessica exclaimed. "I see Amy in her wheelchair and Cynthia is there with her. I also see Herr Mendelssohn, the sweet man, basking in Tempest's glory. Liz is there right behind them, talking with her groom."

They showed the security guard their identity badges, then approached Liz.

Liz spotted them right away and waved, sporting a huge grin on her face. "Jess! Michael! I'm so glad you're here. I could not have done this without you, and wanted to make sure you were here to be acknowledged before the international press."

Jessica moved over to Michael and took the sling and sleeping infant from him. "You were the trainer here, Michael. I'll take the baby and stay on the sidelines while you and Liz talk to the press." Michael looked chagrined, but allowed Jessica to stand to the side with Trevor while he and Liz talked to the press. Michael didn't like Jessica being relegated to the sidelines, but in the past few months, she had been confined due to complications that developed late in her pregnancy, then required a cesarean delivery that necessitated her recuperating at home rather than accompanying him on his trips to the US to help Liz train Tempest. At least Michael had ensured he was home for Jessica's labor and delivery, and was there in person to welcome his son into the world.

Liz was well aware of Jessica's situation, so before talking to the press, she approached Jessica and peered at the sleeping infant. "He's beautiful, Jess. You're so lucky." Jessica beamed with pride, then she and Michael exchanged a look of such love and devotion that the sight made Liz's heart constrict. These two truly loved each other wholeheartedly.

"I hate to do this, Jess," Liz said, "but I have to steal Michael away for a few minutes to help me deal with these reporters."

"Sure, Liz, no problem." Jessica smiled. "Just make sure you return him when you're done."

Liz and Michael joined the press corps and Jessica looked on.

Seeing Jessica standing alone with the baby on the sidelines, Herr Mendelssohn approached her and filled her in on their latest collaboration. Without Michael's knowledge, Jessica and Mendelssohn had been talking, and Mendelssohn had learned through his dressage breeding connections that Michael's former mount, Romeo, had sired a colt, now nearly three years old, that looked extremely promising. Mendelssohn, at Jessica's urging, had been quietly making inquiries about the colt, and was encouraged by what he was hearing. Based upon Mendelssohn's assurances, Jessica was exploring establishing a syndicate of buyers that could help her purchase the colt for Michael. If Jessica was successful and Michael was as successful with the colt as he was with Romeo, they could use his success to establish their own breeding farm, which would support them and their family out into the future.

From what Mendelssohn had just told her, all was going just as they planned. With any luck, she should be able to inform Michael of her surprise in just a few weeks. She smiled her gratitude at Mendelssohn, and hoped the Michael didn't interpret too much into their interaction. Seconds later, when Jessica wasn't looking, Mendelssohn caught Michael's eye and winked at him. Michael surreptitiously winked back.

Michael sat next to Liz during her interview, interjecting occasionally when asked a direct question, but in the back of his mind he quietly reflected on his plans, still secret, to get Jessica back into competition. Liz had approached him out of Jessica's hearing and told him that she had decided she didn't want to continue to compete at the international level after the World Cup. However, she and Michael both knew that Tempest was still in great shape, and could continue to compete and could easily be competitive for the next Olympic Games in two years. Michael had suggested to Herr Mendelssohn that if Liz were to retire from competition, he would suggest that Jessica be the rider to compete Tempest from that time forward. Mendelssohn had loved the idea, but Michael hadn't approached Jessica with it yet. He didn't doubt that Jessica would be thrilled to compete Tempest. The two of them had obviously developed a rapport during their time together at Michael's farm, and if she were worried about leaving the baby, Michael and Trevor would travel with her wherever she would be competing, so they would continue to be together as a family. Michael, Liz, and Mendelssohn planned to speak with the USET about their plans in the next few days. He expected the Team would go along with their plans, especially since Jessica's status as a Team member would naturally bring Michael along as a trainer. His acknowledged success as a rider, then as a trainer with Liz and Tempest, had established him as an asset any country's dressage team would covet.

Michael smiled to himself as he looked at Jessica gazing with motherly love and pride at their son, and reflected back over all that had happened in the last year.

First, after learning from Lionel how he had tricked Emma into believing that Michael was unfaithful to her, Michael had contacted Emma and related Lionel's confession. Emma was shocked, but grateful to Michael for telling her, and apologized profusely to him for not believing him despite the evidence Lionel had created. Michael assured her that he understood how she must have felt given what Lionel had done, it was more than reasonable to draw the conclusions she had, and he even secured an invitation for himself and Jessica to Emma's upcoming wedding to her footballer boyfriend.

Next, there were some complications with Jessica's pregnancy, but everything had worked out perfectly. In addition, the private investigator that Ian's attorney had hired was able to locate the mysterious woman in the bar that had witnessed what happened and she had agreed to talk to the police, who in turn talked the prosecutor, who decided to drop the manslaughter charges against Ian. Unfortunately, the woman's willingness to testify made her a target for some very unsavory people, and Ian was called into action to help her to deal with the fallout. As a result, the two of them seemed to be developing a very close relationship, which seemed very serious.

Lionel was even more successful in his thoroughbred rehabilitation business, and was dating a man seriously for the first time since Nigel's passing. His future seemed bright as well,

Hailey graduated high school with honors in Ohio, and moved to the UK to live with Michael and Jessica until she could decide what to do with the rest of her life. It was a Godsend having Hailey around during Jessica's late pregnancy and post-birthing complications since Michael was traveling so much, so that situation also worked out to all of their advantage.

Michael and Jessica's recent success had made it possible for Hailey to get the more advanced prosthetics she needed, and the change in her was amazing. Now that she could move about without difficulty, Hailey's approach to the life and the outside world had changed dramatically in the best possible way. He looked forward to seeing what the future held for her. As the interview concluded, Michael looked again at Jessica and Herr Mendelssohn talking together. He sincerely hoped Mendelssohn could keep a secret.